AF223131

The Prince in Switzerland

Legacy Love and Pride

by

Dalita I. Alex

TOM I

About the Author

Dalita Alex is of Armenian heritage; she lived on different foreign lands, of diverse culture, from East to West. Since few decades she is living in Switzerland, which inspired her to write these series of books on the history of legacy and root. She holds a BA in history and philosophy, and speaks 8 languages one of them being Japanese.

Her keen sense of writing was apparent at a very early stage in her life and materialized itself during her high school and college years, when she published many of her articles and poems to a broad audience.

In the last few years, she has also written articles on various topics, on health and beauty, and mainly conferring on ethnic minorities.

Her ultimate aim and endowment is to introduce her Armenian legacy to her adopted nation, Switzerland,and to the generations to come.

Besides being an established author, she is also a fervent entrepreneur dealing with pearls, promoting her own line of beauty products.

Her publications also include *Ageless and   China the Pearl and I* translated in French and Chinese.

Edited & proof read by Norman Price, Manuscript Appraisal

The picture on the cover is ARTHUR A. ALEX

The photo of Cross stone, KHATCHKAR,

covered with rosette and botanical motifs with the Armenian Alphabet.

They are found mainly in Armenia and Anatolian regions.

.

© 2010 Dalita I. Alex All Rights Reserved

Manufactured and published by
Books on Demand GmbH, Norderstedt, Germany

ISBN: 978-3-8391-7444-9

The Prince in Switzerland

*To my son Arthur
who inspired me with his princely stance
to write this book*

"I should like to see any power in this world destroy this race,
    this small tribe of unimportant people
Whose history is ended,
Whose wars have been fought and lost,
Whose structures have crumbled,
Whose literature is unread,
Whose music is unheard, and
Whose prayers are no more answered.
Go ahead destroy this race!
Destroy Armenia! See if you can do it. Send them from their homes into the desert. Let them have neither bread nor water. Burn their homes and churches. Then,
See if they will not laugh again,
See if they will not sing and pray again.
For, when two of them meet anywhere in the world,
See if they will not create a new Armenia.

—William Saroyan

Why this book?

All my adult life I was destined to live in different foreign lands; lands of diverse cultures: the Middle East, Japan, China, South America, and the USA. I ended up at the heart of Europe, in Switzerland, where I still live, after several decades.

My identity was never a problem, as long as I was not involved in the core of the system. Whenever questioned about my origins, I would reply in a few words, usually only enough to satisfy thecuriosity or ignorance of the questioner, though sometimes giving a rather more detailed lecture!

It is not easy to be ignored or not totally accepted as an individual. I want others to acknowledge the whereabouts, the values and aspirations, as well as the virtues of those Armenians, who brought their knowledge, enthusiasm, savoir-faire, and positive contribution to the lives of people around them.

I raised my children with an Armenian spirit while reminding them of their sacred duty to honour and respect their new homeland, Switzerland. When I first arrived on these shores, Armenians were neither well known nor numerous. For most Swiss, we were a small ethnic group from the Caucasus, dispersed around the world, and they knew little of our national history. It was because of the Armenian genocide that newspapers wrote about us, and the Swiss were more or less acquainted with the Armenian question, the massacres and deportations perpetrated by the Ottoman Turks in 1915. However, that was virtually all they knew about us and they did not known much else about our past history or rich identity! This was despite the fact that Armenians had enriched all the countries they lived in. They bestowed in many nations, throughout decades, their cultural, scientific and literary contributions.

The present-day, Swiss-Armenian citizens reside mostly in the French-speaking canton, mainly in Geneva and Lausanne, which enjoys many different and active Swiss-Armenian associations. The Armenian Diocese gathers all Armenians from German and as well as French and Italien cantons. Armenian philanthropy built the Apostolic Armenian church of Sourp Hagop at Troinex (Saint Jacob). The pastor of the church gathers a few thousand Armenians in his uplifting religious *badarak,* (church ceremony).

The case of the Germanic canton is another story.

Zurich, asthe centre, does not have a large Armenian community.We have to keep up with religious commemorations on a quarter-yearly basis, and since we do not own an Armenian church, our reverend priest has to conduct the most awe-inspiring, overwhelming religious services, the heritage of 1700 years old Ecumenical rite of sacrament, heartening our religious and national spirit through the Hymns, nostalgic chants and melodies, awakening memories of our past heritage in a number of different sister churches.

I took the initiative to contribute in my own modest way. Unfaltering and resolute, I was determined to tell the story of a migrating, roaming, and journeying Armenian people. My intention was to enlighten, inform, and entertain the younger generation, non-Armenian - acquaintances, contacts and readers alike - about the identity, the achievements, and contribution of the Armenian peoples past and present, and explain the reasons behind the shaping and underpinning of the Armenian Diaspora!

I created a protagonist whose status as a prince at the beginning of the 21st century denotes the lineage, tradition, and the cultural values of the Armenians. He is the fruit of a mixed marriage of Swiss-Armenian parents. His leading role of ancestry consolidates a conceivable identity of Armenian history, which, for so many centuries has symbolised the roots, love and the integration of its people as sustained by them faithfully to the threshold of the third millennium. My protagonist is the direct voice, the fruit, the inheritor of praiseworthy, valiant soldiers, *sbarabeds, nakharars* (generals, lords) and kings, who have struggled for so many centuries, paving the history not only of the Armenians, but also playing a role in the history of neighbouring countries and feudal states. They fought terrible and powerful foes for the preservation of their Christian faith and for the freedom of their land. Effectively, my protagonist carries the characteristics of Armenian men, rich or poor: intellectuals, businessmen, scientists, traders and peasants. Armenian men at the threshold of the 21st century are like my protagonist, whom I have named Hrant (a homage to Hrant Dink). They are committed princes, and like their ancestors, live with the age-old aspirations for peaceful integration and acceptance with remarkable tenacity and fortitude. Devoted souls, bound to their heritage, and endlessly pre-occupied with their own survival and progress under many banners and languages.

My protagonists, far from being imaginary, are similar in many ways to the people around me. Nonetheless, my purpose was not to re-write the history of the Armenians. I am simply conveying what I have experienced through my ethnic inheritance and through my personal research over the past few years. In this effort I am indebted to the works of many eminent historians, philosophers, and writers.

In memory of Hrant Dink
The martyred Prince

Armenian dispersed in neighbouring lands mainly Asia Minor,
ME, Europe America. They have migrated across the fve continents.

Mr.Charles Aznavour, the very prestigious , esteemed and honoured artist,
author and composer, recently Ambassador of Armenia in Switzerland,
has once said you can find Armenians in every corner of the world,
even in Maw Maw, a far stretched city in Africa!

Administrative map of Caucasus in USSR, 1952-1991

Contents

The Empire of Tigran the Great, 95-66 B.C.

Empires come and go; however the greatness of their achievements and the significance of their legacy are emblazoned in their progenitors.

These men are the priesthood of an oppressed and noble nation. It would be difficult, perhaps, to find the annals of a nation less stained with crimes than the Armenians, whose virtues have been those of a peace, and their vices those of compulsion. But whatever may have been their destiny… their country must ever be one of the most interesting on the globe; and perhaps their language only requires to be more studied to become more attractive."

—Lord Byron about Armenians

The Prince in
Switzerland

Part I

The Random Appointment

Hrant

'What's your name son?' Doctor Grimm asked the young man sitting in front of him in the first class compartment of the TGV train bound for Paris

'Hrant, sir,' was the swift answer of the young man.

'Allow me to introduce myself, I am Dr Grimm from Zurich.' The doctor offered Hrant his hand and gazed at the lad. Dark haired, with large brown eyes, he was a handsome young man of about twenty and some years, he concluded with his penetrating, insightful assessment. The young man's big dark eyes, alert and piercing, yet exuding kindness, reminded him of the Caucasian look, but the refined features left him perplexed. The young man was wide shouldered; robust but not that tall, he decided, an assumption considering they were both seated at the time. He had a wide smooth forehead with no etched lines of wisdom, and a straight nose, which ended with a short obtuse tip. When he laughed, one noticed his well-aligned white teeth, protected by voluptuous lips above a manly chin. Even though physiognomy assumes ethnical or national traits, our nosy Dr Grimm was unable to advance much in his conjecture. He frowned. 'Hrant you said. What origin does this name have?'

The young man, dextrous and nimble, leant towards his inquisitive travelling companion. Now it was his turn to inspect the middle-aged man, who was growing ever more curious and impatient for a reply. 'I am Swiss-Armenian,' he announced proudly.

'Really? I could easily have taken you for an Italian or from the Baltic regions,' said Dr Grimm, this time his reply in German, after having first spoken to Hrant in English.

'Well, yes, I suppose sometimes that's the look I project,' came Hrant's prompt reply, as if he had anticipated the question and the answer was in his thoughts, in his mind, in his genes, deeply rooted in his DNA and mostly in his heart. It is like a push button; the moment you linger and touch any of such unusual inquisitive questions, but then you should regret maybe for being so curious. All these kind of eventful and critical curiosities can be overbearing, annoying or ill felt, if not dealt with finesse and proper accent

Dr. Grimm smiled, respecting the ensuing silence of Hrant, who seemed in a very profound state of mind. Even though the young man has no lines of wisdom on his youngish forehead, he certainly has the sparkle of intelligence in his eyes. 'But your name Hrant,' goes on our curious Dr Grimm, 'is it a Swiss name? I have never heard it before.'

'Well, no,' explained Hrant with respect towards the elderly man's undeniable interest which, to a certain extent, did not bear a forceful inquisitiveness, as Hrant had first thought, but rather had a note of warmth and friendliness. 'It's an ancestral name, coming from past centuries. Actually I am named after my great grandfather. But a full and detailed explanation of the origin may take too long, which is why I cannot fully satisfy your curiosity, I'm afraid. Suffice to say, sir, I am a living monument,' Hrant added with a smile, 'I carry in me the traits of many generations. My ancestors were mostly Armenians, sometimes inter-married with different nationalities, mostly Latin, all carrying their heritage with pride. We are people who speak several languages, assimilated in different cultures and ethnic groups. In addition, as I am the progenitor and the result of mixed marriages, actually I carry a third name, which is Jean. I have many cousins, named after their grandfather or father: such as David, Omar, Elizabeth, Nicola, Dikran, Edward, Aram, and George, to name only a few. I think Hrant Bagratuni Schulthess sounds too far apart, but that is the beauty; I carry the paradox of difference, which brings about resemblance. I have a direct lineage of kings and princes of Armenia; say Armenia Minor or Kingdom of Cilicia, and the kings of Bagratuni. The dynasty's sole purpose was survival among different emerging powers and feudal groups. Various kings, nakharars, barons and generals paved and opened doors, thus bridging the gap between the East and the West. They were daring and committed people, implementing strong boundaries of munificence and allegiance. They were modern people of their times – daring men of vision and inspiration who aspired to develop a better environment. Their intelligence and far-sightedness promoted and encouraged creativity and scholarly resourcefulness. They were builders of churches and fortresses, enhancing to the welfare and culture of the area, encouraging and fostering agriculture to combat famine, and the development of medicines to combat major sicknesses such as bubonic plague and cholera, which would wipe-out a whole town, leaving disaster and mourning. They encouraged commerce, the trading of spices, silk and precious stones, between Asia Minor, India and Europe. Some historians have acknowledged and praised them for their ability as rulers, and for their efforts in promoting peace within the region.'

'Bagratuni?' Dr Grimm whispered to himself. Mesmerised and speechless, he remained silent for a moment or two and gazed again at Hrant. Who is this young man? Why does he know so much? Why was his response to the question so prompt? 'Mr Bagratuni,' he said at last, 'do you have a business card? I would very much like to have your phone number, and of course I will give you mine.'

During this relatively brief encounter he had been very impressed by this young man.

The professor

Hrant reached into a rear pocket of his jeans and produced a rather crinkled business card, which he offered to Dr Grimm with more than a hint of embarrassment, regretting his oversight in not carrying new business cards on him.

The doctor took out his wallet and extracted a pristine card which read:

Dr. Walter Grimm

Professor in History at the University of Zurich.

There was also an address in Kusnacht - nicknamed the "Gold Coast" - an elegant suburb on the shores of Lake Zurich. Dr Grimm was not only a curious man; he was also a man of knowledge, someone who looked for detailed answers to questions. He always tried to dig deep in his historical research. Initially he had written his thesis on Middle Eastern history. Everything he had read or learned for his doctorate, all of his dedicated research, was documented and shelved in his library. He was presently researching the direct descent of some of the protagonists Hrant had mentioned; those who had shaped history, thus drawing the political religious and social structure of their times.

Now our professor was again listening to young Hrant, carefully and judicially, without interrupting him. Here was a living specimen from the far end of Asia Minor. This young man belonged to an ancient nation, owing an inscribed history of some three thousand years. Hrant, the professor realized, was a mine of gold, a roomful of history sitting there in front of him, yet so handsome and juvenile, full of youth and intelligence. What a blessed day, he thought gratefully, a day where he was encountering a living history coming directly from ancient roots of Caucasus.

The card said Hrant Hetoum Jean Bagratuni Schulthess. These names were strangers to the professor's ears. Names that are remarkable and too far apart, names with atypical, miscellaneous roots polcs apart. 'Bagratuni!' he repeated loudly.

'Yes, professor,' went on Hrant, with his overwhelmingly passionate accent. My mother is Swiss, from the Schulthess family, the German speaking part, from Canton de Lucerne, and my father is an Armenian born in Geneva. He speaks several languages. As I have told you, I carry the name of my grandfather, which is a traditional tribute, especially when I am the only male of the family. As for my second name, Hetoum, it was the name of one of our kings, my ancestor, in the thirteenth century during the Cilician kingdom (in today's Turkey). King Hetoum was a handsome, strong, vigorous person. History praises him as a wise, intrepid and trustworthy king. He brought prosperity and peace to an unstable

18

area for several decades. His reign was longer than any other king in the Cilician kingdom.

'I see,' said the professor, a smile teasing the corner of his mouth. 'Well, Hrant, may I call you by your first name?'

'Oh yes, of course, professor.'

'I will try to call you in the coming week; you must come to meet me, then we will continue this passionate historical conversation at my home. I'm hoping you will tell me all about your past in some detail. But right at this moment there is a question which is burning my tongue.'

'Go ahead, Professor. Please ask.'

'Well I am curious to know the initial reason why you ended up in Switzerland, effectively nicknamed as the land of "Milk and Money". Why are you, a knowledgeable young Swiss of very rooted Armenian heritage, living so far away from your homeland?'

'Dr. Grimm, your broad insight, sir, could eventually bring forth this culminant question of our presence in distant lands, far from the land of our memories and the dwelling places of our ancestors. My ancestors have looked for a sacred haven for so many centuries, roaming on different lands. My family's ship has accosted the Helvetica land! I am the pedigree, from my father side, of noble kingdoms in the Near East, the Armenian kingdom of Cilicia, which lasted for three hundred years, from 1078-1375, and to the Bagratuni kingdom from 885-1045, areas covering Mount Ararat in today's Turkey. After the fall of the kingdoms, Armenian kings could not re-establish themselves and their sovereignty. Having lost their kingdoms and feudal states, they were depleted, becoming the pray of incessant invasions. They fought for centuries with different feudal lords, caliphs, sultans, emperors, and khans, forced to live under the rule of Arabs, the Mongols, the Byzantine, Turkmen, the Persians and ultimately under the Ottoman Empire. Henceforth, the aristocracy had to find refuge on different lands, to escape the harsh situations implemented in the area. They wanted to go back to greater Armenia, I am sure. But there, too, they were vassals to

Tartars, Arabs, and then the Turkic tribes, of unsettled powers. Each invader deployed, implemented, and drew a new boundary for Armenia. The last invaders and occupiers around the 20th century were the Ottoman Turks and the Russians, the main protagonists, who bargained on the Armenian lands to expand and proliferate their political advantages.'

Dr. Grimm nodded knowingly. 'That is true.'

Hrant said, 'the first Republic of Armenia, endorsed, and deployed by Russia, America and big European powers, implemented an independent Armenia from 1918-1920. It bordered Georgia to the north, Ottoman Empire to the west, and Persian Empire to the south, and Azerbaijan to the east. The republic covered most of the present-day Armenia, plus the regions around Mount Ararat Kars, and Ardahan districts, while the regions of Nakhchivan, Zangezur, and Qazakh were disputed and fought over with Azerbaijan. It was the Ottoman Empire's aim, especially during the World War I, to erase Armenia completely from the map, to link his territory to Azerbaijan! The Russian Tsarists, and later on the Bolsheviks, my dear professor, tried to protect Armenians, defending them against the Ottomans and the nationalist Turks. The Russians endorsed through many treaties, especially the Treaty of Sèvre in 1920, defined to protect the Armenian borders. Unfortunately, until today, the dispute on Nagorno Karabagh (lands regained by Armenians) has not ended, Azeri claiming the Armenians ancestral lands back. Armenia gained its final independence for the second time only recently in 1991 after the collapse of the Soviet Socialist Federal Republic.' Hrant paused and smiled. 'I am more than proud that today Armenia has taken its place as part of the nations of the world. Even though a small, humble nation, rising up from its ashes, it is a free, Christian country which deserves the attention and respect of other nations big or small.'

'Indeed.'

'Dear Dr. Grimm, our history is full of wars and unrest. Armenians in the West as well as in the East were to bear and endure all kinds of invasions, persecution, massacres, harassment, illiteracy, poverty, and nature's fury too, the 1988 earthquake in Armenia. Through centuries, they had to bear contemptuous attitudes towards their language and status as foreigners. They had to bear physical and moral tortures, and were subjected to undemocratic, discriminative attitudes, subjugated, encroached, and depleted; most of the time levelled to a secondary citizenship. These xenophobic attitudes were not targeted only towards Armenians; it was and still is a living pertinent social problem faced by innumerable ethnical and minority groups.'

The professor nodded in understanding, and Hrant went on, 'One has to remember that we been mainly divided into small principalities after the fall of the Cilician kingdom. The same situation beset the Armenians in their motherland, where most of the natives tried to run to escape the persecution, political instability, enduring suppression and lack of freedom, and of course the terrible poverty. They were looking for safe havens and strong governments, so neighbouring countries - Iran, Jordan, Lebanon, Syria, Iraq, Russia, Ukraine, Georgia, Crimea, Poland - and most European countries - America North and South, Canada and Australia, Africa north and south - were the lands where Armenians took refuge. They were hoping for the sun to rise over their homeland, to eventually return to where they belonged, back to their origin, the land of their ancestors, the land of their history. They shared a compulsion to hear again their clear, crystal brooks, their red soil full of their foot prints, their uneven fields packed with multicolour flowers, surrounded by herbs of precious medical elixir, dancing through the sweet breeze, orchestrated by the song of birds, Mount Ararat taking pride in the valiant home-comers. I think it is the obligation of our generation, with the means of intellectual and scientific probe, to bring light and correction, where there is darkness and lies.'

'I am most eager to hear more of your recital, my boy,' exclaimed the professor, unable to mask his excitement. 'I have read unaccountable history books, in enormous libraries, opened archives, read about wars, treaties and mischief. Read on royal succession, royal marriages, but I have hardly met a living history like yours. You look to me as if you came out from a museum or a video that has captured main events, and sequences of the centuries. How discerning and significant this must be, just knowing to which tree you belong, drawing your ancestral accounts and portrayals, to be a forefather, grandson and son of an ancestral tree, and mostly, my dear Hrant, to feel proud of those particular and prerequisite stages.'

'Effectively, incessant wars and political instability, my dear professor, and the destruction of our kingdom were the major reasons that induced Armenian folks, rich and poor, aristocrat and simple folk, to disperse through centuries to different lands and establish new havens for their offspring. Yes, they crossed snowy mountains, hot deserts full of snakes, and stormy seas, to find safe havens. They continue to challenge their destiny, trying to accept their intricate heritage, at home, or in Diaspora.'

The professor was watching Hrant's charismatic face, scrutinising his eyes that were speaking of love, compassion, hate, war, and peace. They were carrying beams of happiness and sorrow, agony and ecstasy, freedom and survival, bearing and witnessing all humanity. Hrant's eyes were the unbounded messengers, conveying the future, of their future, projecting as far as our blue planet shall scribe for its progenitors, to meet other stars, other cosmic habitations, to implement the heritage of lived and thrived reminiscences, and conclusive recollections of mankind.

Mia Culpa my Love

Hrant was now in his new compartment. He did not have much hand luggage, no burden to weigh him down. He was light and young, a bachelor in love, enjoying his freedom and comfort. He never carried much luggage anyhow. He had his laptop and some reading material with him, and a plastic bag very neatly lying alongside his chair. And a package attractively wrapped, a box of Swiss praline for his friend's family.

Actually, the Swiss are famous for their chocolates. A man named Emile Frey from the French section (Romanch) of Switzerland, started mixing milk to chocolate, a homogenous mixture of cacao powder and cacao butter; a succulent concoction and a tasty outcome, which is a major denominator of this successful and famous business of Swiss chocolate in the world, like Nestlé, and Sprugly to name but two. Belgian chocolates are also famous. They played a prominent role in the chocolate industry by introducing the praline chocolates, filled with all kind of creams and fruit-based fillings. I think chocolates, regardless of their source, have a powerful impact on our emotions.

Well, our boy Hrant needed to carry his emotions, translated in every piece of praline. The message was very clear and obvious - lots of bites of love, amen! He also had two bottles of fine Swiss wine from the Wallis, a canton west of Switzerland. The wines were from the region of the Rhone River valley, which is protected by the Alp Mountains. These wines are renowned for their fruity light taste - especially the Merlot, Dent Blanche, and Chardonnay.

Hrant's choice was for the red wine of Pinot Noir and Dent Blanche - these bottles intended for the father of his beloved Sara. He had been travelling for almost two hours. Along the aisle, one row in front, sat a little girl with dark brown hair, neatly and beautifully attired in a cotton dress, with lace and satin ribbons all around the collar of the dress. She was a comely mixture of innocence and class, around eight year of age already a French adolescent. A Swiss girl at her age would wear only a simple trouser with a tricot or oversized T-shirt. French say: "L'habit ne fait pas le Moines" and Germans say "Kleider macht Leute" both of which translated, denote explicitly that outer appearance does influence to a certain extent, an onlooker's opinion of an individual's status. Well, at least in Hrant's case, he could guess that the little girl was not Swiss. So it does reflect at some point, perhaps, the outer resonance.

He put down his book and closed his eyes, letting some peace cradle his mind. In a meditating mood, he recalled the speedy events that were to change, and confront his very existence. Some few months back he had met Sara at a dinner party hosted by Alain, a renowned artist/painter in Paris, an enthusiast Armenian in his sixties. Among the guests were Mihran and his wife Sophia. Sara was their daughter.

Alain had pioneered the circle of Armenian intellectuals and artists. His aim was to meet occasionally with people, to discuss their latest achievements or to introduce another eminent artist, a newcomer to their friendly circle.

Hrant was the newcomer, though not an intellectual in the true sense of the word. Initiated into the circle as a patrician of nobility and gentry with the ascendancy of the Armenian lineage. He was being acknowledged and praised by his French milieu for his elite upper class, princely status. His status as an aristocrat was to denote lineage, tradition, and survival. He was a strong advocate of the Armenian-folk and their cultural values. He was a prince without a chateau, or fortress, nor any political authority. He was without a devoted army under his command, and neither did he enjoy the colossal richness of some kings and royalties of this world. He did not have the power to decree laws, nor revolutionize, amend or reshape history. But for Armenians, rank denoted something different. It had another connotation; it stood as a symbol of historical continuity, the offshoot, and the pride for ongoing heritage and fraternal bondage. Hrant's enlightened character was an inspiration for the new generation, standing out and manifest in every gathering of Alain and his friends. The French-Armenian circles cherished his presence.

Hrant-Hetoum-Jean was carrying the names of his eminent ancestors, the ones who drew history, manipulated events, and were responsible for shaking, shaping and paving the destiny of the Armenian nation. He stood for the direct descent of those praiseworthy Armenian kings, becoming the voice and the vestige of a legitimate past, the living token of a historical pride. As the remnant of those kingdoms, he was the bridge, which was to bind six hundred years of history.

His simplicity and warmth typified the Swiss-Armenian. His Swiss entity gave him a more ponderous relaxed attitude, a more pragmatic stance, watching at events, and grasping the reality of the times with matter-of-fact, rational attitude. Belonging to a minority pushed him towards understanding and sharing other origins. He was well aware who he was, and conceded by accepting a colossal responsibility. His aim was to devote and use all his energy towards one goal, the revival of a foreordained path, consecrated and commissioned to bring light and order to his roots, by highlighting the remnants of his past.

He could well be American-Armenian or Belgian-Armenian, British-Armenian or Arab-Armenian, but his insight, judgement and cognition would not deter his convictions and respect towards his legacy, the gratification and dignity of belonging to an ethnical group, the pride of a very old nation that played its importance in history. He was aware and complacent to his title, and all the weight that title bore to his young person.

His blood boiled for the love of his country; his inbred strength and intelligence were the dominant factors in his personality. He was a supporter of conciliation and order. His friends from all over the world were his inspiration. He had a heart for giving, sharing, open to arguments, ready to respond and be responsible. He was an inspiring and innovative young man, living with the realities of his time. He was aware of the world's globalisation problem. However, his optimal goal and objective was to find recognition and well-established justice for the Armenian cause. That night he met many other young Armenians like Vahé, Varoujan and George, all brilliant young men like him, incontestable lovers of culture and beauty. Alain's circle and their frequent meetings achieved the desires of these youngsters. Hrant was becoming the cradle of their growing inspiration, each occasion enhancing the opportunity of bondage and amity.

Notwithstanding this, Switzerland was to remain and prevail as his inherent and constitutional terra firma. He was born nourished of its conservative and orderly environment, a superb milieu between the green meadows and sparkling winter snows. It was his doting and caring homeland, actual and factual. He had acquired the Swiss sense of order and simplicity, and understood and accepted their hard and pragmatic militant attitude; and shared their values of neutrality and democracy. It was a Swiss perspective, since the foundation of the Swiss Federation 1848. They implemented very strongly their political vision of Direct Democracy in political and social issues. Notwithstanding he carried his Swiss identity along with his Armenian aristocratic descend, very comfortably and in conformity.

The train was announcing its arrival at the station of Gare St Lazar. Hrant woke up and looked around. The seats were almost empty; the little girl in the laced dress was not there! He instantly regretted missing an opportunity to bid her goodbye. Amazed at his long sleep, he leapt to his feet and reached for his belongings, determined not to miss his arrival to Paris.

From the station platform, he looked for the taxi exit. He stood there patiently in a queue. Mihran had told him to call when he arrived at the station, but he felt more relaxed not to bother him, knowing the commuting system in Paris was like all big cities, time consuming. For him, Paris was a city close to his heart. He spoke French fluently; it was his third 'mother' tongue, after Switzer Dutch (Swiss German) and Armenian, the language of his soul, which he practised with his father and grandmother.

At last he was in a taxi heading to district 16, a very elegant district of Paris. But on arriving at his destination he was overcome by a feeling of uneasiness. All his cheer and enthusiasm waned. He started sweating at the idea of his encounter with Sara after a long break.

Mihran and Sophia

Hrant was now in the corridor of a very nice apartment, on the second floor of the building. A very friendly voice welcomed him from the loudspeaker on the apartment's porch. Even if one did not understand Armenian, one could grasp the tone, the resonance of sweet surprise and joy. 'Oh! At last you have arrived. Vertchabes hassak.' These two words denoted all the love, respect, and attention that an Armenian could show to welcome a friend.

'Hello, Sophia,' was Hrant's reply.

They hugged each other warmly. Two decades separated their age, but their true feelings were of two friends who had missed each other. Hrant was not very adroit when it came to such delicate moments, but Sophia was someone special. The couple were his father's best friend and, of course, the parents of Sara! Actually, Sara was the replica of her mother, only two decades apart. Sophia had a more mature look, which did nothing to diffuse her ageless beauty. She was a charming and sweet person. Sara, so like her mother, was the most beautiful, comely person ever.

Sophia was almost singing out of happiness; she could not hide her enthusiasm. She was very happy and overwhelmed to see Hrant. 'It has been such a long time since we last met,' she went on in a half scolding, half teasing tone. 'You look good, as handsome as ever.'

Hrant wanted to respond in full diffidence, but was given no chance. She went on, saying: 'everyone agrees with me; there's no secret about it. You are a charismatic person, full of compassion.'

'Thank you, Sophia' was Hrant's muted response as he eyed the floor to hide his embarrassment.

'Mihran and Sara are not here yet. They won't be late. You saw how busy are the streets of Paris. Commuting is so difficult; he was expecting to come and pick you up.'

'Oh yes I know, I did not want to bother him. He had also proposed to send one of his employees to meet me at the station, but I don't like to trouble him. That's the Scorpion, my astral sign, which has a significant influence on my behaviour in general. My star is that of a prince with a very humble conspicuous stance. I do not like to take advantage of my friend's kindness, nor impose my person. I am a prince only for those who acknowledge it, committed to critical positions on different issues. My dear Sophia,' continued Hrant in one breath, 'neither do I boast, assess or make use of my title to raise the ego of some of my acquaintances.' He followed this with a burst of youthful laughter.

'Yes we know by now, my dear Hrant. We are aware of your truthful motivation, your endeavour and concept towards sharing and assuming the recognition of your heritage. Your aim is to obtain the gratitude of your rank on behalf of your nation. However, take it from me, you are, and you belong to a very old aristocracy, and that reality you cannot change by not paying heed! It is not you who fashioned it. It was given to you as a heritage. So if I were you, I would take it and make a cross on my heart.' She, too, then succumbed to laughter. 'Now tell me how is Igor and your mother, our Lady Maria. I miss her too. You mentioned on the phone that they would join you in a few days time. They have an important appointment in Liechtenstein, I believe?"

'Yes, I think they were invited by the prince consort to attend a classical concert at the theatre of the palace. It's a pity they're not here right now, but I am sure we will have many occasions in the future to all be together.'

'I do hope so. Now, would you care for a drink or a coffee? I have espresso, our French style coffee; or if you care, Armenian coffee?'

'Hum, Armenian coffee! Well, Sophia, let's go for the Armenian coffee, I am surprised that you still use it.'

'In fact, my employee, or rather my right hand, comes from Beirut, she knows and still uses most of our ancestral customs. She is the one who started once again the use of Armenian coffee. I had the coffee pot in copper from Yerevan. All we had to do was purchase the very finely grounded Arabica from the Armenian supermarket, and the rest was taken care of by Anna.'

'Oh Anna, yes of course, I met her. She was here last time when I visited you. How is she? I will be happy to meet her again.'

Anna was a young woman in her late thirties. Robust with thick brown hair driven at the back of her head, revealing her moon face and fading complexion, like the pale light of the moon, hidden behind thick summer clouds.

'After the Lebanese civil war,' explained Sophia, 'she lost her husband, shot dead by a sniper. She was a widow left alone with a son of just eight years old at that time. Anna had found Mrs Aznavourian through friends. It was a very difficult period for her. She had to face and accept the loss of her loved one, and cope with her desperate financial situation, the major reason that made her leave Beirut, the city where she was born and raised. She has now worked for the Aznavourian family for ten years. She cares about them like her own family; the only family I have she concludes with pride. I love Sara like my own daughter, and Madame Sophia is a jewel, a true lady. She gave me shelter and love. I am very lucky God in his mercy did not forget me.'

Hrant was reminded of the attitude of man, and his urge for war. The aftermath of such wars was always devastation and human loss. He said, 'I reckon that is the destiny of the Armenian people. Their love and attachment to their homeland or the lands they have migrated. They are builders, pacific souls that assess and value life. So often, in their history, they have found their homes destroyed either by war, looting, or prowling criminals. Brainwashed chauvinist men, filled with blind hatred aimed at destruction, leaving only remorse and sadness, and undeniably distressing memories in the hearts of the bearers.'

There was a noise at the entrance door and Anna hurried to open it. Mihran was on the doorway of the living room. Vigorous shaking and hugging were the speechless gestures that Mihran and Hrant mutually shared. Sophia with sparkling eyes, was blessing this happy moment, witnessing the hugging and embracing of two men that she cared for most.

'Where is Sara?' was the first question of Mihran to his wife.

'I am sorry I was late.'

'At what time did you reserve the restaurant, sirelis?' (*My sweet in Armenian.*)

'At eight,' came the reply.

'So, we still have some time left,' said Mihran. 'We can chat with my dear friend. Meanwhile you can offer us an aperitif before we leave. We have to drink to celebrate the return of our friend Hrant.'

With Sara not yet home, Sophia started to show signs of impatience. She tried many times to call her on her mobile, to no avail. She waited a while before going into the living room to tell her husband and guest that Sara seemed not to be joining them tonight, since it was almost time for them to leave, if they don't want to be late for the restaurant. 'Besides,' she said, turning to Hrant, 'I am sure you must be tired and hungry. We really must go. I will leave a note for Sara, with the phone number and address of the restaurant. Hopefully she will join us later.'

Hrant had no chance to object. He would have preferred to wait for Sara. He stood up to go to wash and refresh himself. Mihran wanted to freshen up too. So for some time the house was silent, except for the sound of water singing a joyful tune, and the murmur of Sophia's voice overplaying the running water's cool and clean sigh - to Mihran's ear like a bee wheezing to the calyx of a flower, before sucking its nectar for her honey.

'I am ready,' Sophia soon called, surprised not to find her husband in the living room. 'Usually men are faster getting ready on time,' she added, 'but I think he is an exception.' All this was said with a teasing smile on her beautiful face. But to her surprise, Mihran was standing behind her, shaved, and dressed up in jeans and a very attractive shirt with vivid colours, giving more light and a younger look to his tired face.

'But Mihran,' asked Sophia 'why are you in jeans? Do you not know where we are going? You need to wear a tie; it is the rule of the restaurant!'

'Well, my darling,' Mihran said, looking pointedly at Hrant, 'you will have to change your restaurant. Since, neither Hrant nor I want to be dressed up. We want to enjoy each other and converse casually on so many subjects that are burning our hearts, and rendering our minds impatient. We have so much to say; I am sure Hrant agrees with me. And for that we need to be comfortable.'

Seizing the chance, Hrant expressed his preference to stay at their home, and settle for a more modest meal, some food that maybe Anna could prepare. One of Anna's magic Armenian dishes that he had missed so much.

Mihran was all in favour of his suggestion. 'My wife had a brilliant idea, but it will be better if we do it tomorrow, would it not, Sophia?

All this was decided so quickly that Sophia had no chance to disagree. Instead, she merely smiled, which emphasised her striking beauty. Her makeup and apparel, chosen with such exquisite care, boosted her femininity. She was wearing a very elegant, well-cut, black velvet suit; her diamonds and pearl earrings were adding more sparkle to her pale face. The river of pearls on her neck, like Venus's tear drop before meeting her loved one, was exquisitely caressing her soft skin, thus bringing up the contrast of her black suit. Paris was and is the capital of art culture and fashion. All big designers and artists introduced and displayed their creations in Paris. Therefore, it is a well-established fact that the Parisian women go with the inspiring fashions, inspiring agelessness and beauty.

On the other hand, Mihran of course was an exception to this trend. He had a classy taste. Effectively fashion and livelihood implements a deep social anchorage, the tools to express creativity, class, or manifestation of any kind of rebellion dealing the new generation!

Hrant was breathless in front of such a beauty. Swiss women are not so elegantly dressed to go to a restaurant. To choose sophisticated make-up, or a fancy toilette like this, they need events that are more important. As for the jewels, they hardly wear anything, other than perhaps a small diamond or a gold ring, the simplest possible. It is very unusual for a Swiss woman to own large items of jewellery, and even if they do, they seldom dare to show it to their friends," for some reason that has a deep-rooted social issue.

My mother, thought Hrant silently, has everything like Sophia - beautiful dresses and very old pieces of jewellery that would turn people pale with envy - but she hardly ever wore them. They are family tokens would be his mother's excuse. She feels proud to look at them and then return all these treasure back, in a thirty cubic cm deposit box at the bank. These jewels are the token of our families. Beautiful tiaras, designed for distinctive heads: confined to princesses and royal breeds, to instigate the concept of power, pride, and strength. It was a vow of devotion, to care, to protect and serve the crown's integrity. A burden, a sacred and blessed commitment, solicited and assessed by the aristocracy and the people, to endorse and substantiate, reinforce and validate the Armenian kingship till the end. A responsibility that each of the crowned heads had undertaken, to carry these tokens with humility and honour. They had to rule and serve with devotion, thus to protect their country and their fellow brethren. Over many decades these jewels, worn by the Armenian aristocracy, became more emblematic, denoting pride and lineage. They symbolized a representation of richness and power, for princesses without a kingdom, having lost most of their subjects. They became exemplifications and vivid proof of a glorious past. They were legacies, inherent treasures of grace and magnificence.

Sophia was indeed a committed woman, knowing when and where to impose her feminine power, a delicate person, to enchant and glorify her husband. She thought men more pragmatic. For her, this was a game that she played with ease and class; no hard feelings, not even the slightest remorse. She was already out to the kitchen to look for Anna. Anna was thrilled at the news. She was happy to serve a prince. In any case, Anna was used to unexpected dine and wine impositions. Her cupboards and refrigerator were full for such surprising, unplanned dinners.

The clock on the wall broke the brief silence by striking nine. It was time to stand up, to satiate, and gratify empty stomachs.

Sophia returned shortly to announce that dinner was to serve. She had changed into another beautiful dress, of dark green satin, matching her almond-shaped, brown eyes.

Mihran and Hrant rose and walked together into the large dining room.

Opulence, class and tradition

The spacious dinning room had a classical décor. A magnificent chandelier, ornate with Baccarat crystals and many tens of bulbs, illuminated the room. Good taste and privileged décor were welcoming Hrant, inspiring but not intimidating for our prince, who grew up in similar environment as a young man. Nonetheless, his taste was so different today. He was Swiss on matters of taste and simplicity. He had a very modern living room with leather sofa and a dining room with simple natural wood table and chairs. He looked more for utility than luxury, simple lines in a comfortable environment. He was happy and touched that Sophia had brought out all of her beautiful china to honour her special guest. The tableware exuded class and beauty, but was not ostentatious. Her intention was clear; she was simply anxious to please him.

The exquisite aroma of the lavish *mesa (Lebanese)* term of a collection of dishes made with *chickpeas Tahine, aubergine, Bulgur* and all kind of salty pastry filled with cheese, meat and spinach, salads with plenty of parsley and tomato, to name a few. All this variety of food was prepared in the interval of one hour. Anna was undeniably a great cook, a master of her profession. Hrant was overwhelmed; everything smelled good and tasted exquisitely delicious. He smiled, thinking of a popular proverb: Tell me what you eat, I'll tell you who you are.

Well, he liked everything that was on the table. He enjoyed every bite. The smell of the food reminded him of his childhood, of places he had been with his father. He recalled their visit to some second cousins, scattered around the globe, where he ate such Near Eastern food! And now he was eating and drinking, merrily like a king, surrounded by his minister and his wife, while expressing his enthusiasm to the lady of the house and her chef. Suddenly he had a pang of concern. Sara had not arrived. Where was she?

Her parents had not fully explained her absence. 'Sara is her own girl now,' Mihran said. 'She is free like a bird to decide her own future, with neither obligation nor any restraints. Unlike other youngsters of her time, she could have chosen to live all by herself. She is our only child, so we solicited her to live with us, to enjoy her as often as possible, sharing her everyday life. Moreover, she had no objection to our solicitude. She is attending Sorbonne University, preparing for her Master in Sociology. She is a brilliant student,' the proud father would point out from time to time.

Hrant had the same view and impression as Sara's father. He found Sara not only charming and attractive but very knowledgeable, curious, up to date with the problems of our world. Many subjects were close to her heart, like her origin, which she praised, even though she was very French, (having a French father and an Armenian mother) a nation that loved Armenians, and had historical ties, especially in the 11th century with the Crusaders, to the present time.

As the big clock struck eleven, Hrant felt a sensation of fatigue; he had eaten more than was normal for him. Temptation had befallen him; his brain had failed to inhibit his gourmet delight. This was a night of celebration with real friends, a carpe diem. The CD was playing softly: Aram Khatchadourian's Guayane suite.

Hrant had indulged in the delights of a bottle of *"Chateau Neuf du Pape"*, a millissime of the best cuvée. It was a full-bodied wine, almost as old as his birth year, which gave an invigorating sensation to his palate. Each time he took a sip of that fantastic scarlet liquid; the lingering effects of aftertaste had a voluptuous affect in his mouth.

The tone of the telephone stirred him from his somnolent state. Mihran had picked up the phone. He had been expecting that call for a while, it seemed, for from time to time he had been glimpsing at his watch. Hrant had noticed those glimpses for the same reason, Sara! She was apologising for not being with them. She could not come home, even though she knew that Hrant was going to come from Switzerland. What was her excuse? Exams...! Well that was enough for an excuse. At least it was a plausible one.

Part II

Back to reality

In his somnolent state Hrant started to think back. What had kept him from seeing Sara over the last few months? There had been times when he was not able to show up, unable to keep promised appointments. But was he truly that busy?

He stood up to refresh himself in the bathroom, to splash his face with the running cold water. He combed his dark brown hair, very neatly cut, drawn straight back as befitting a noble man, alluring and charismatic. Was it really some four months back that he had been to Paris to the Alain's banquet dinner? It was a circle that had heightened his soul, meeting a group of eminent French–Armenian scholars, and politicians, people of light and integrity, gathered there on a common ground, to share the love of their roots and their compulsion for an enhanced and fulfilled tomorrow! He had meet Sara on that beautiful Parisian night, along with her parents.

She was in a very casual dress. A pretty face, with smooth lines, where one could notice the buds of youth; pimples, scattered here and there on her face, giving her a more charming and youthful look. Her most eye-catching feature was her thick healthy brown hair, shiny, with smooth waves, covering her slender shoulders, thus framing her large brown eyes. A strait nose, very characteristic of her heritage, graced her face, while her high cheeks overlooked a voluptuous mouth. Features so distinguished and matching, all on a fair face, like the drawing of Botichelli's painting, who had gone with all his artistry and his ingenious brush, to reveal God's incomparable creation, the woman. A very fine neck bridged a slender body, in harmony with the features of her face. She had the perfect silhouette to make women envious, and bring men to her feet. He recalled how their eyes had met, their prolonged and earnest eye game, full of wonder and consideration. God she was lovely!

Who is this handsome, elegant person who was shaking hands with every one? She had wondered. Her father was introducing him to the guests; and to her mother, who was smiling proudly like the queen butterfly. She had waited patiently. She knew her turn was to come. She was the daughter, so either she was to be the first or the last. In any case that was not the point, the culminating issue, which was eating her up, was curiosity, an issue making her somehow perplexed and impatient. What made father so complacent, filled with pride, trying to introduce that young man of almost her age, to elderly people, who were bowing as they were introduced to him?

At last Mihran reaches his daughter. 'Sara *sirelis*, this is Hrant,' was his voice in a pressed but sweet tone, proud of his gesture, condescending and disdainful, sure of his coup.

A moment of great consequence was taking place, pre-ordained by fate. It was a pre-destined moment in time, inscribed on their lifeline. Two beautiful souls, assigned, were shaking hands for the first time. If Hrant were a nimbus and Sara a cumulus, the thunder, the lightning, the electric shock provoked by them would bring tonnes of pearly rain from the sky, ravishing and watering thirsty meadows and fields. Hrant and Sara were soul mates; they formed the most beautiful picture ever. Sophia was thrilled, delighted, and unable to take her eyes away from them. They were still holding hands when Mihran came and whispered to Hrant, 'Come my boy, there is a very eminent person who wants to meet you.'

The cosmic magic of the moon

It was late evening when Hrant and Sara had the chance to meet once more. They sat at a bar, like youngsters of their age, all formality left aside, open, and uninhibited, trying to elaborate their friendship, without any prejudice, informal and easy. Their education was of different branches. His was in the financial world, at the heart of a rich country like Switzerland, having the German language for his everyday use. Hers was in the sphere of sociology and philosophy, in a powerful country like France, practicing French for her everyday life. Nonetheless, they both spoke Armenian, if not all the time, but they grasped it fluently. They were concerned, partisan of the same issues. Their purpose in life was of the same direction, of the same bearing. They were predisposed to bring good around them by advocating the pursuit of the right and integrity. They sat talking for hours about their respective parents, their schooling, and of love!

Sara had had few boyfriends in the past, nothing serious, she told him, her cheeks red under his penetrating gaze. 'They all wanted only one thing, free sex,' she said forcefully. However, her concept of life was more earnest; she believed sex without love was like food without spice. She wanted to marry the person of her heart, and she was very portentous about that issue. Even though she felt emancipated, she disapproved most of the behaviours of the society, which was rapidly undergoing so many changes. Many words were losing their power or concept, like the words honour, moral, class, to name but a few. They both admitted that globalisation was not only engulfing the economic and financial system, but also sweeping up the social structure and scheme of things in Western society.

She went on about protecting youth, since she said they are not being given all the opportunities and support they need. On the other hand, Hrant was somehow reticent about the way modern parents treated their children, pandering to all their desires. Ungrateful children most of the time, efforts of parents committed to colossal sacrifices, to assess and comply with their children's desire, was not always compensated for, nor did it find its merit!

'If I bear children, I will act moderately,' Sara said, looking straight into Hrant's eye, which became bright and illuminated at this statement.

'So you would like to have children?' was Hrant's happy reply.

'Of course, I would like to have many children,' insisted Sara. 'I was raised as a unique child with no brothers or sisters. A house is empty without the laughter of children. Besides, they are our progenitors, without them our lives would be selfish, thinking and working only for one purpose, the "I", and that is not what I yearn for and hanker after! Women who love their partners want to bear the children of their loved one, bearing the fruit of their love.' She paused and gave him a sweet, grave glance. Was that the look of women in love? At that moment she was aware of her own heartbeat, and that made her even more uneasy and timid.

Hrant remained silent, entranced by this young charming lady, intelligent and attractive, sitting there in front on him. He was under her spell, bewitched and wordless like a little boy lost in wonder. And this Armenian Aurora made everything so perfect for him. 'Dear Sara,' he said at last, 'I would like to know more about the insight of a modern French Armenian, to become aware of your concept of life. I do already feel that we are on the same wavelength on almost all issues, especially your concept about the realities of our world, regarding love, sex and marriage.' Choosing his words carefully, he went on, 'our society has changed; moral issues are not perceived like they were some generations ago. We are much unconstrained, liberated from formalities, not to forget the stance of women emancipated. Today's generation, especially in the developed world, is fancy-free to choose, to enjoy an unrestrained style of life. Notwithstanding we are more responsible in our choices, trying to learn from our own mistakes, even though the price to pay is sometimes so high. But those are our experiences, sometimes good, sometimes unaccomplished, unrealistic experiences, but freehanded, bold and audacious. We are ready to reckon the aftermath of our decisions and acts, and not to blame either parents or society.'

This monologue was followed by a more prolonged silence, until Sara mentioned that she felt the need for some fresh air. They had been sitting there for a long time, and Hrant, too, was beginning to find the room's warm atmosphere rather stifling, although he was too polite to speak first. But he swiftly agreed, so with a sweet smile, Sara fetched her bag and her jacket, and then followed Hrant, happy and a little tipsy, to the door. They walked out of the bar.

Something unexpected had occurred; their open unconstrained discussions had created a kind of intimacy. They walked silently side by side for some time, admiring the cloudless sky. Stars were shining over their heads. It was the crescent moon, the moon of wishes. 'It is an old oriental superstition,' Sara was telling Hrant in a funny voice, not totally convinced of her tale, 'that after you first glance at the crescent, you must make a wish and stare into the face of a person whom you think will bring good luck to you for the coming months.'

Hrant laughed aloud. Why not, he pondered. This was his chance, regardless of the content of the tale, and assuming that the action would be louder than words, self-rewarding. Amused, a big smile on his face, he followed Sara's instruction. He closed his eyes, turned his gaze to the crescent moon, and then, before opening his eyes, turned his gaze straight towards Sara's face. She was there, all illuminated by the light shed from the street bulbs. He perceived her face, caught sight of her beautiful, distinguished eyes, and in that momentous second he emulsified and suspended into her unfathomable soul. It was a heart-warming and emotional moment of fascination that rendered him speechless, a momentous occasions that the moon had bestowed him. The moon's energy, the impetus of great consequence, its magnetic force that governs the tides, its power on the universe; a force beyond logic, beyond anything felt or lived by him. He was so stimulated and electrified that he abandoned all restraint. He planted a gentle kiss on her forehead; others on her cheeks, then spontaneously fetched her mouth, to give a bigger and sweeter kiss on her rosy lips. Sara was also bewitched, under the spell of the moment. She offered no resistance; all of her senses too were melting under the heat of the crescent moon. Superstition or not, it had already enhanced a bestowal of luck and good fortune. Some gestures talk more than hundreds of words. It was so spontaneous that Sara had no time to realise what was happening. Thrilled and overjoyed, she could neither move nor open her eyes. She remained motionless, not knowing what was the next step.

At last she opened her eyes to see that Hrant, so bright and condescending, was now like a fearful child, cognizant and sensible, to realise his gesture. He drew back, taking a step backward, watching Sara's reaction. They were both silent now. What went on was a reaction of enticement and captivation. There was no blame, nor reproach. It was tribute, a glory to the drawing power of the moon and the magnetic attraction of the momentum, enhancing the alibi and the exoneration.

So many times after, he had seen the crescent, hanging up in the sky. He had closed his eyes to think of Sara and her comely eyes, so innocently looking at him; and then recalling the instant of the sweet kiss, a taste so intense, so luring, to shake his whole being, alerting all his hormones and make him kneel to the moment's absolute commendation.

Their farewell was that of two friends who got along so well. They promised they were to write and visit each other frequently. He was in love, desperately in love. However, paradoxically his letters were telling of his itineraries, rather than alluding of his love and care. He promised to meet her as soon as he finished some of his duties. Well, regrettably, he had not kept his promise. Was it too late for him to repair his mistake?

Reckoning his regrets

When Hrant re-entered the room there was an almost total silence in the house, broken only by the softly muffled tones of Anna and Sophia mixed to the clinking sound of cutlery and porcelains, mingled to the timbre of emptied crystals cups.

Mihran and Hrant were a little tipsy, and eager to elongate the night. Under the spell of this bewitched scarlet liquid, singing and praising friendship, youth, beauty, and love.

Outside, the Paris breeze was swirling the windows, with a scent of fresh air trying to wash away the reflection of the full moon on the windowpanes. From high in the sky the two gleaming stars of Hrant and Sara were illuminating the whole hallway. Although the couple were not together again yet!

Minutes had elapsed, when Hrant finally returned to the living room to find Mihran waiting for him. 'Hrant my son, you have to taste a cognac, a very special Armenian cognac I brought from Yerevan last year, when Sophia and I were invited for a forum of

Armenian Doctors.' He showed him the big fauteuil, and Hrant, like a son to a father, nodded his head for the cognac. Only the glug...glug as the liquid caressed the crystal cut glass permeated the comfortably brief silence.

'To your health,' said Hrant to Mihran.

'To our lasting friendship,' echoed Mihran, meeting Hrant's warm gaze.

Words had no place there; they might even not accomplish the truth or be explanatory. But the eyes cannot lie; they can only reveal the truth. And now Hrant's eyes were asking Mihran, 'Where is Sara?'

Mihran inhaled deeply, then said, 'The phone was Sara.' He paused momentarily, then explained, 'She is giving all her hearty excuses for not being able to join us tonight. She was with a few friends working on her thesis.'

There was again a very profound silence. They were both very much absorbed in their thoughts, each trying to analyse the situation from a different angle. They both new what the other guessed; they both knew they loved the same person on different levels, of different kinship, and cared for her presence dearly, ardently, affectionately!

Sara's seat had been reserved on that elegant dinning table for quite some time, until Anna guessed that Sara wouldn't be coming.

'A thesis needs serious preparation,' remarked Hrant, to break the silence. 'I remember my own hectic days at the university, back at *Sengal*, while preparing for my Master's degree in Economics. I fully understand Sara's situation. She must have much research to undertake in her sociology courses.'

'You know, Hrant,' - this time Mihran was leading the talk - 'I am very happy that she is preparing her thesis on ethnic and race relations, social psychology and sociology of gender, which will enable her to deepen her knowledge of the Armenian people, radically, regarding yesterday and today. By studying the social construction and stratification of our race, she will gain more empirical insight, and become equipped to reconsider some of the questions concerning our lineage, such as: discrimination, migration, social change, class justice or injustice, as well as economical, political and cultural structures.

Hrant nodded. 'Yes, sociology or social sciences is actually a term derived from the Latin word *socius* (companion) and the Greek *logos* (knowledge). August Comte, the father of sociology, thought to unify all studies of humankind such as history and philosophy. He believed that all human life passed through the same distinct historical stages in theology, metaphysics, and positive science. If the individual could grasp their progress, they could prescribe the remedies for their society. Of course, this is a theory that cannot be functional to all issue and in all fields.' After a short reflection, Hrant went on: 'indeed it will provide Sara the deep knowledge required in resolving some of our social problems. In addition, she will be able to trace the origin and growth of our social classes, by analysing the influence of group activities on individual members, having in mind the fact that we are very individualist people.'

Suddenly they shared a burst of laughter for getting so emotional and having so much expectation of Sara's future achievements.

Passion pegged to love, like the thorns of the red roses,

After his hearty thanks for a splendid evening, Hrant took his leave from Mihran and Sophia. A taxi drove him to *George V*.

It was well past midnight when he got to his decorous hotel room; he felt deeply fatigued. Undressed and sleepy, he slid between the spacious bed's perfumed, clean sheets. The chiffon-like embrace of the soft and satiny covers caused him to imagine the wonder of Sara's soft caress. He knew she had punished him, her absence stood for so many words. He tried to close his eyes, for the illusion of the moment, to feel the sensual touch of his beloved Sara's satin scarf, a token from their last meeting. For weeks, he was dreaming of her, his hormones were failing him; his nerves were throbbing at the thought of her comely face. The fragrance of her perfume on the red scarf awakened his senses more than ever, standing as the epitome and the embodiment of her sweet being. Oh, Sara, how I miss you. His memories well awake, his senses incited, sent fire through his body, thrust like the thorn of scarlet roses. A ravenous desire was overwhelming his being. In a drowsy state he sat on the side of his bed, took his face in his hands, cheerless and moody. When he then looked around him, everything was nice and orderly, but it stood as alien and unwelcoming. He stood up and crossed to the refrigerator for a glass of iced water. Returning to sit on the edge of the bed, he tried to analyse the evening he had with Mihran. Actually, it was already yesterday; the clock of a near-by church was striking two.

'I have to sleep,' he said, voicing the thought aloud. 'Tomorrow is an important day, and my agenda is full.' He threw himself, naked, in to the immaculate sheets of the bed. The touch of the soft sheets raised in him the sensation of abundance and rest. The red scarf, ensnarled on his chest, was like a serene, gentle whisper, cradling all night long, his gloomy, enamoured soul. His manly chest, sprinkled with abundant hair, emphasising his masculine look, was suffocating under the pressure of his feelings. His heartbeat was pounding so wildly that the whole room was feeling the resonance, the nimble energy of a young man in love.

Hrant did not see the sunrise; he was at last sleeping soundly, the night was long, imprinted with love. His handsome male figure, like Michael Angelo's David, was laying sound sleep, lost in the fantasy of his dreams. Nature was generous when it had shaped his features - not only was he born with a crown on his head, he had also inherited the best genes, acquired the best features of both parents. Effectively they had bestowed him with the handsome head and the vigorous shoulders to carry that crown. Hrant was, without doubt, a handsome guy with outstanding physical characteristics to bring any woman to his bed. This fact was not a secret to him. Women were attracted to his outlook. He was a classy and attractive male. A very important privilege, considering the world which he was facing.

Real men are becoming scarcer, considering all the social and sociological upheavals that our world is going through. Men are no longer that gallant and do not relish the full responsibility of caring for their women, the way old generations did. It is a race, which is gradually vanishing.

The liberation of women in society and the balance of power between men and women has paved a new understanding regarding sex, relationships, and marriage. Men have to assume their new position, making some concessions. They now have to accept women as their equal. Honestly, they cannot achieve equality on the same issues, since each fulfil and enhance in the other their relative weaknesses and strengths. Their respective roles need to be redefined.

The sun was shining on Hrant's face, the rays so strong that their touch was stinging his delicate eyelids. He did not move he was savouring that cosmic heat. The intensity of the pricking rays was like a goad, to stimulate his sleepy being. Gradually he was feeling too hot; he could not stay under his satin blanket any longer. He jumped out of bed and looked for his watch. It was time for him to move. The sun was already high in the sky, and he smiled, thinking the impelling force of the sun's rays had driven him out of his bed. The classically furnished bedroom was bathed in a white light, soothing his strong headache. From his balcony he looked down at le Champs-Elysées, which is already throbbing with life. He had to hurry, if he wanted to be on time for his appointment.

Dining in privilege

Mihran was on time, waiting for him in the luxurious lobby of the hotel. He gave a big hug again, as if they just met. Were they not together only the night before? But warm hugs are customary for people of Caucasian origin. They sat on one of the comfortable nineteenth century sofas at the *La galleries*, which is the heart of the hotel. It was so beautifully furnished with 19th century paintings and furniture, and the walls covered by Flemish tapestries. There were showcases full of antique pieces, while artful statues of naked maidens revived the royal atmosphere, while adding to the sensation and privilege of being in the presence of elegance and good taste. Looking around, one could spot people of certain standing, either tourists, or natives playing the host by inviting guests, to boast of their city's fine hotels, the classy taste of past heritage, of pride and refinement.

They were there to plan the details of Hrant's week. Mihran had to take him to the club, then Hrant had to visit the national Library, to look for an archive. Inexorably every now and then he was waiting to hear when and where was he going to meet Sara. Mihran could not quite grasp Hrant's aching desire. His politeness and reserve prevented the young prince from voicing his burning concern. He sat there listening to Mihran, meanwhile ordered an aperitif to soften his throat. He called for a *Martini*, while Mihran, loyal to his caprices, opted for a *Chivas Regale* on the rocks.

'Actually tomorrow night we are going to Maxim's and I hope Sara will join us, but nothing is predictable with youngsters; one has to be careful. You are an exception, my dear Hrant - with you I have no age problem, since you are such a mature guy; people of any age can have a pleasant and fruitful time in your company.

Hrant was again in the clouds, thinking of the possible restaurant meeting with Sara. Why can I not call her just to say hello? What went wrong? Had he been too passive last time they met? Was Sara really attracted to him, or may be fallen out? All kind of supposition and hypothesis, a brainstorming, brought a lump to his throat, a tight squeeze that made him feel uncomfortable. He wanted to loosen his tie, but that would alert Mihran to his mental turmoil.

He leaned back on the sofa and gave a deep sigh. Mihran, who was busy writing on his agenda, had noticed only that Hrant appeared to be daydreaming. Meanwhile, like God's ordained accommodation, Mihran was soon busy answering phone calls. Left alone in his abstract preoccupied state, Hrant was striving to return to a semblance of reality, to his role of a host.

The dining room of *George V* was exquisite, effectively deserving the three stars Michelin award. It had one of the best French gourmet restaurants, along with wine at its best. A three star menu for a light lunch ordained and prepared by the best French chef, notwithstanding in a very privileged and elegant milieu. The chairs were in grey and gold colour, while the tables were dressed with the best tablecloths, china and silverware, all created specifically for the hotel. The menu was light and tasty:

Royal Style Chestnuts with Black Truffles

Frog Legs with Jerusalem Artichokes & Herbs.

Medallion of Veal with Capers from Pantelleria.

Roast Wood Pigeon from Landis with a Turnip Sauerkraut & Basque style Juice.

Soufflé Columbian

Coffee and Tart à discretion.

How delightful it all was! It was a work of art in excellence. Sitting there, they could enjoy the hotel's courtyard and garden. Spring was there in all its majesty, adding to the impression of enjoying a fine lunch in one of the France's Chateaux. The weather was perfect and the flowers were so vivid and abundant, completing an image of peace and beauty.

Hrant could not sustain nor hold his dismay; he could not even hide his sadness for not seeing Sara. Silence was king considering his moody attitude!

Mihran, seeing his friend's absent-minded state, decided to adopt a fatherly role: 'Did you talk to your parents? Are they coming to the ball on our Benevolent Night, for the young artists of Armenia?'

Our prince nodded for a yes, then in a voice full of emotion said, 'I wish Sara were with us, as well as Sophia.'

'Yes, Sara should had been here with us.'

'Time is running out, I have so much to do once I return to Zurich. Unfortunately, I do not know when we can meet again.'

Mihran gave a paternal smile. He had understood already during the dinner last evening that the moment was right for this couple to meet. Like a father to a son, he calmed him down by saying, 'My dear Hrant, don't worry my boy, tomorrow night I am very sure she will come.'

But there were many uncertainties hanging in the air.

Sara's dilemma and dismay

Sara had watched three crescents and two full moons, thinking and passionately waiting for Hrant. She was confused and bewildered. He had written to her describing a recent visit to Venice, and had mentioned his yearning to be with her on his next trip. Venice is a true romantic city, he had said, a city where the renaissance period mingles with the contemporary time. She picked up his letter and proceeded to read his passionate words:

My Beloved Sara,

I am dreaming of the moment we will be together, my darling, sitting in the Gondola side-by-side, hand in hand, one heart one soul, to be cradled on the Venetian waters on a beautiful hot summer night. To be watched only by the sparkling stars, with a flawless, unfathomable cosmic horizon as our heavenly shelter. As for the blessed moon, which is solemnly keeping my secret wishes, to be revealed only upon fulfilment. However, my dearly loved, I was there not to enjoy the gondolas, nor to discover and enjoy the beauty of Venice, nor its artwork by renowned painters. I was there to continue on the Island of San Lazar, a Mekhitarist monastery.

The Mekhitarist monastery has been there since the middle ages. Father Mekhitar Appa founded it around the seventeenth century. They have contributed so much to the Armenian culture and education, consolidating the Armenian contribution in the fields of letters and sciences, in philosophy and religion.

I was well led by the monks, who are residing in the monastery. I saw their library full of antique books in Armenian, and Latin scrolls some six to seven hundred years old. It is like encountering all the intellect of the past in one space. They were the ones who printed the first book in the sixteenth century. I learned about the visit of the English poet Lord Byron during the 19th century, who helped the Armenian monks to pre-

pare an Armenian-English grammar book, printed in England.

Lord Byron not only learned the Armenian language, but was also fascinated by the character and virtue of the Armenian people. I will tell you more when we meet about the Mekhitarist and their contribution. They are the scrupulous, gratified witnesses of our past and present. Not only I am impressed of their achievements, also I can wholeheartedly confirm their august bestowal. In one word, it is an affirmation and manifest evidence of the heritage of the Armenian wisdom. Inevitably, it is the benevolent and intellectual contribution of its people at the heart of Europe.

Sara paused to dwell on his words. She was more than thankful to her parents for having raised her with the desire and hope of redressing and redefining her identity in the current world.

Hrant's letters were another substantiation, reckoning the attention of nations, communities, and social groups to the influence of the Armenians and their important role they had played in human history and socio-geology. A bestowal that was mainly undertaken under harsh situations. Over the centuries they have contributed greatly in such varied fields as religion, medical science, mathematics, architecture, and business – resulting also in many and cultural enhancements. After reading Hrant's letters, Sara felt as if she was sitting on a cloud. She had met the man of her life, a precious soul, and a vestige from the past, but with very modern and pragmatic ideas. He was an intelligent, mature prince among men, brimful of ambitions. She was so much in love, but she could not find the right words to express herself. Effectively, their friendship was not developing on the sentimental issues. All she had received from him was a warm kiss under the spell of the moon. Oh how she had savoured the honey-like taste of that one sweet kiss, but it was so little to drench her overwhelmed feelings. She wanted to satiate her feelings and gratify her soul's delight, to pacify and mollify the aches she was feeling deep inside her body. She was now living the memory of those nostalgic moments.

Oh Hrant, Hrant where are you? -Yes (talking to herself) - I am angry, and impatient, discontented because you have not been able to keep up with your promise. You are running out of your pledge, making the lapses between our encounters, stalking and lugging. Perhaps I am asking too much. I think you do not love me as much as I love you!

A very feminine way of perception would ponder Hrant if he had heard her monologue. Women in general have a different approach when treating and analysing events, sometimes they do not act with objectivity or balance their passion rationally. True love needs time to prove itself; sacrifices to endure in its fulfilment, to reckon and to comply with different issues. Love needs to build strong pillars, to enhance fulfilment and recognition, thus manifest a bestowal of consolation.

The memories of their cheerful loving moments distracted her completely, by drawing her attention away from her studies and her close friends, especially Christian and Juliet. Christian was attracted to her since childhood. For Sara he was a classmate, a childhood friend. They had chosen the same courses, which led to them sharing many moments together, while preparing for their exams. Christian was of a bourgeois French family. His father held a senior management position in a food-processing factory. Effectively, it was Hrant who had captured Sara's heart and soul. She was sure he was the man of her life, the prince of her heart. And her feminine intuition was not wrong in this matter. She was acutely aware of the fact that an electric arrow had pierced her delicate heart, and something irrevocable had taken place in her mind. She was sure that she was to carry his heart in her forever. Their minds were already merging harmoniously through the quantum waves of cosmic energy, blessed by the light of their unbounded sparkling stars.

During many long days, and sleepless nights, she has been awaiting a phone call from him. Instead, she received short emails with short sentences to tell her about his job and his undertakings. Seldom would he mention any word making or alluding to their relationship, or referring to her beauty. His only concern about her, were her studies, and her well-being. He would conclude much love and greetings to her parents! Every now and then promising to meet her as soon as possible, making the intervals shorter; promises that he had not fulfilled, from the time he had last left Zurich.

The way to gratify love, is love itself

Hrant, thinking back on his own attitude, mouthed a sad smile. He had at last comprehended that he had not acted according to his promises. He had given his word to call upon Sara, while ensuing almost the impression that he was not respecting his promises. In his letters and e-mails to her, he had not shown any particular affection fondness or warmth. He was always on his guard, discreet and prudent, hiding and controlling his true feelings, purposely skipping appointments and postponing dates, finding this or that excuse to bring down the fire and control his upheaval. Inevitably, she was the woman of his heart. He was terribly attracted to her, and he was so much in love, something that he had not felt before with his other dates. He had felt her heartbeats on his chest. Her feeling of affection had stirred his soul, inspiring and moving his free Apollo spirit.

He had had some romantic adventures, firstly with schoolmates, and later within the university circle, where he had met some beautiful girls, intelligent, ambitious, but those were like a dawn's short promise. Nothing serious sprung from those relationships, they were all short-run affairs – pleasant but temporary encounters that served to broaden his experiences of women. These brief love affairs helped him to understand, observe and sense more the feminine gender, which was quite complicated, he soon realised. As his mother had told him: 'to have a harmonious and long-lasting relationship, besides love, one has to understand that there should be some concessions from both sides. We are not the same in our education or character; nobody is perfect. Marriage is a matter of give and take. When personalities are involved, character and behaviour are major denominators in a lasting relationship.

However, first, and utmost is the chemistry that plays the first major role. That inexplicable sensation that we call attraction, love!'

'Sara,' he would tell his mother, 'is my ardent choice, the woman of my life. Oh yes by God! She was waiting for me. How foolish of me! I knew that she is the woman of my dreams, of my yearning, yet I played the imbecile, always too reserved!'

'Well, its never too late, my son,' came his mother's measured reply. 'So what are you waiting for? Introduce her, this choice of your heart, to your father and me.'

Love verses prejudice

Living with mixed-up feelings of regrets and yearning, he recalled the cherished moments when he was with Sara. He evoked the moment he had held her in his arms, having felt the pressure of her breast, and light and swirling, touching his body. He had the sensation at that moment that both were melting in each other's soul, taken in completely, incorporated, becoming one. It was as though nothing else mattered. The warmth of their passion gave them the sensation that they were illuminated embodiments, like fireflies living the divine magic of their fate, happenstance of a moment in time. When they were together, time and space became irrelevant, immaterial. Love was in the air, passion all around and felicity in their future.

Hrant's education had much to do with his behaviour. He thought by keeping his distance before serious engagement was to honour and cherish this lady. His intention was not to hurt her feelings or take advantage of her weaknesses. However, at the threshold of the 21st century, all this kind of gallantry and these sanctions on passionate, amorous feelings were to be underscored. One has to act freely without any prejudice towards relationship. His behaviour and approach was so much out of place, out of his time, he thought to himself. Love must have no excuses; it must have neither boundary nor time. If it knocks at your door, you should open and let it in; you should grasp it in bliss, since it is not given to each and everyone to find true love, to find his or her soul mate. It occurs only once in a lifetime. We are not talking of sexual attraction, which is another kind of love. Indeed, it is an attraction, a very strong happenstance, where the self is targeted and the pleasure of the flesh satiated. But such an act usually has no longevity, like when throwing a stone in the lake, spiral waves ripples and undulates the water around the stone surviving a short while, quick and strong ruffles, but so ephemeral.

Hrant and Sara were lured, captivated to each other like the attraction of the two poles, congruent, inseparable, and forever. Some couples start with sex and reach to love, some start with the feelings of love and compassion to reach to sex.

Part III

Moments in Time

The dinner at Maxim's was set for at eight o'clock. Mihran and his wife were to meet Hrant in front of the George V Hotel. Overjoyed but nervous, thinking of the appointment and perplexed about the tackling of the night.

Hrant wanted to look his best. After a quick shower, he roamed about in his robe. At last he decided to wear his dark brown suit, a very elegant Italian-cut dinner coat, with fine beige stripes. A very modern, yet classic suit, he had bought it with his father, in an elegant shop in Milan. He finally found a matching shirt with an off-white high collar to go well with a red necktie. He drew a perfect picture of a gentleman jumping out of a fashion magazine.

Looking at himself in the mirror, he liked what he saw. It was effectively a narcissist attempt, but in that prevailing moment, he needed that; psychologically he was in a whirlpool of emotions. In his mind, for that special rendezvous, nothing was more important than his appearance, neither his important diplomas nor his ancestral title. He wanted to impress and surprise Sara with his look. Sara was living at the heart of youth in and around the campus, and had herself been raised in a cultured environment of class and beauty, so he had to impress her at last with his real privileges. He regretted his less than pro-active role in fostering and developing his relationship with her. However, he was now willing to bestow to his beloved woman, at last to declare his passionate affection and love, without any reserve or prejudice. He was ready to undertake and convince her of his warm feelings, to maker her aware of the true depth of his tender passion and devotion.

All such kind of thoughts drew him to look his best and by God he did. It was not difficult, since the elements at hand were already there, and all he had to do was to assemble them correctly. There was the same worry when dressing the table; you hand out to lay your table for special occasions, with exquisite lace cloth, overlaying and using all your best china, cutlery and crystal glasses, to brighten and sophisticate your guests. He even took one rose bud from an arrangement in his room, and pinned it on the right side of his dinner jacket. This was the name of the game. He glanced again in the mirror and found some red blotches encircling his eyes. He sighed; there was nothing he could do about that. But otherwise all was looking well.

Mihran and Sophia were waiting in the glamorous lobby of the hotel, ostentatious with its artful flower arrangements, displayed in every corner. Their classy presence was completing the main attraction of the imposing lobby. Hrant spotted the two of them in the middle of the milling clients. What class, he thought to himself; they were his future parents-in-law? – He dearly hoped so! He walked briskly towards them, privileged and pleased to be with them.

Mihran smiled and offered the prince his hand. 'Hrant my son, I hope you did not have to wait too long. You know we Armenians, we are always late to our appointments, whereas you, the Swiss, are so punctual.' As for British they array punctuality as one of their highest virtue".

Hrant expressed his utmost respect to Sophia by laying a delicate kiss on her hand. She felt charmed encountering a royal inherent. She looked like a true lady herself, coming out of a renaissance picture. The couple looked happy and relaxed. Hrant, on the other hand, felt disappointed at not seeing Sara with them.

Sophia was the first to bring up the subject. 'Sara will join us at the restaurant,' she said. 'She was late home, and so had no time to be ready on time. Please excuse her for us.'

Hrant was suddenly calm; he looked at Sophia from a man to a woman, weightiness in his voice. 'It's all right… I understand. If you want I can go and pick her up,' he offered readily.

'No, no, my dear Hrant, she can manage by herself - taxis are for that! Besides, the restaurant is not very far from our apartment; we are in the same district.'

They left together via the main entrance. Their car was already there, the key in the hand of the page, who very politely had opened the door to Mihran as well as to Sophia. Hrant took the back seat. This was a momentous event, an interim occasion. He was heading towards his destiny. He knew it was time to apologise for his sardonic behaviour and tell her about his love and desire. The route to Maxim's seemed unduly long; he was so impatient for this overdue meeting with Sara, and to remedy the mistakes he had made in the past.

'Here we are,' Mihran says at last, breaking the silence in the car. Nobody had uttered a word as, understandingly; they all had one common thought in that car, namely Sara. All three of them - mother, father, and suitor - were deliberating on the same issue, though from slighting different angles.

Their reserved table was in the best corner of the restaurant, and the chef welcomed them in a most gallant way. It was an illustrious, exclusive restaurant to exalt one's appetite with the promise of the finest gourmet cuisine. Luxuries are not necessary, but they are the lace, the illusion of a moment in their reflection. It's "dine and wine" in the harmony of beauty, the rare, and the exalted. Very special menus created accompanied with rare ingredients to satisfy the palate of the very refined clientele. Maxim's cellar boasts the world's best wines, dating from the beginning of the century.

The Aznavourian came from time to time to entertain their distinguished guests. As for Hrant he grew up visiting Maxim's ever since he was a young boy, in the company his father. The menu card did not show any price listing, so sitting in that restaurant one had to forget about price, and think only of his palate's fantasy and caprices.

They started with a cocktail, while awaiting Sara's arrival. Chatting amiably for several minutes, Hrant did not think of Sara, a change of attitude, feeling merrier and relaxed. Since they shared the same outlook and opinions on life, the conversation was cordial and relaxing. Hrant was happy to learn more from elderly persons, and they, in turn, were interested in his more youthful approach regarding the issues at hand.

Suddenly, Mihran smiled broadly on noticing le maitre, who was walking in front of a very elegant beauty. 'Sara,' said Sophia, 'there you are, *Hokis* (my darling), and bravo, you're not that late!

Hrant was flabbergasted. It took him a moment or two to regain his composure and to jump from his chair. She was here! She was even more beautiful than the picture in his mind. Elegant and feminine, she had the allure of a real princess, truer than any authentic painting. She had all the class, the beauty, and the chic in that royal-blue dress. He guessed right away the reason, for her having chosen that special colour, since he had once told her, when asked to name his favourite colour, that he liked all shades of blue, especially the royal blue, which was the emblem of their family. That divulgence spoke for many words, an endearment of delight. Sara was unveiling her fillings, she was confessing her vehemence and compassion openly, She was effectively showing him that she was thinking of him, and her choice of that dress was an open consecration. Upon this revelation he stood up confidant. It needed only a fraction of a second to change the attitude of a man, who had thought that women were the weaker gender!

After Sara made her round, hugging and kissing her parents, Hrant was standing erect behind his chair, patiently waiting his turn. When she reached her seat, he took her arm delicately and sealed a warm kiss on her hand; then slid her chair to seat her comfortably at one of the most prestigious tables of Paris.

He was unable to detach his gaze from Sara. He wanted to whisk her away, to have her all to himself! But no, how about Mihran and Sophia, they are important too; he loved them and never wanted to hurt their feelings. What a crazy and selfish idea! He had wasted so much time; he had to cool down and behave. Yes, of course that is how it is with Armenian gentlemen. Oh father, father, voiced Hrant to himself, your sturdy education and genetic vibes are always inspiring, to esteem and apprehend people of all status, rank, standing or position, and utter respect towards his loved one!

Sara did not talk much; she was rather listening first to her father, and then to Hrant, trying now and then to give her ideas, or querying gently some of the things said, but always playing a supporting role and never trying to lead the conversation. Some allusions were made about Hrant's parents and about the Swiss in general, the weather, and Swiss uniting the European Union.

Sara did not eat much. Neither did Hrant. Sophia was not happy, looking at her daughter's plate. 'Would you prefer to try something else?' asked the worried mother.

Sara smiled sweetly and shook her head. 'No thank you, mother, everything is perfect. But I'm sorry to say I'm not that hungry. As for the wine, I cannot take much, since tomorrow I have a very important exam. I must be at my best for that, so I can't over indulge.'

Suddenly there was silence. Hrant gave a long, loving look and raised his glass. 'Let's drink to Sara's success,' he proposed. Then turning towards her, searching her attractive honey-brown eyes, he said, 'Sara I have missed you so much. Please forgive me for not calling you regularly. Thanks for coming and brightening our evening.'

Upon this declaration, Sara raised her cup and drank to his health. 'I thank you too, my prince.' She blushed and looked down at the table to hide her emotion.

'Your dress is so beautiful and it suits you so much, mademoiselle Sara,' declared Hrant, cheered by Sara's crimson reaction. 'It is the colour of class and power in the Armenian dynasty.'

'Well I do not know about power' goes on Mihran, 'but I know it is a colour that you should wear more often my beauty, *keghetzigess*.

Sara could not wait to be alone with Hrant, but an opportunity such as that was very unlikely to present itself that evening. The semester was to end shortly. She was deeply involved in her studies. On the other hand, Hrant seemed busy with artists, and political personalities. Therefore, they tried to talk on the phone most of the time, waiting impatiently for the big ball, where the two families were going to have a get together.

For Hrant that day was to have another connotation, since he wanted to ask Sara to become his wife.

The ball

'Father, did you have a pleasant flight?' asked Hrant cheerfully. 'Oh mother, you look so lovely. For tonight everything is ready; the Aznavourian's are so impatient to see you both.'

'Yes,' his father said, 'I talked to Mihran and Sophia. I have missed them too. There is going to be many speeches during the ball and Mihran wants me to say something about our family, and the contributions we have made in the Armenian Diaspora.'

'Well, father,' replied Hrant in a teasing voice, 'that's something you adore doing, isn't it?' And then turning to his mother, Maria: 'Mother, tonight I want you to be at your best. I want that everybody sees how beautiful is my mother.'

His mother smiled wistfully. 'I will do my best, son. With all the kilos I have accumulated on my waist I need a miracle!' She paused, then added, 'I am sure Sophia is as slim as ever.'

'Well my delightful mother, you are beautiful the way you are. But I know that a dress is a second skin for a woman and a way to express her feelings, her emotions. And if I know my mother, she has already meticulously prepared.'

'Hrant, Hrant my sweet and charming boy.' She gave him a hug before turning to her husband. 'You know, Igor, our son is more radiant than ever; did you see his eyes?'

Igor glanced at his son, and then with an amusing smile turned to Maria. 'He has the same eyes as me when I was dating you!'

Their shared laughter made Hrant swell with happiness. His parents had not met the Aznavourians since the occasion of their anniversary, when Sara was just twenty. He was so looking forward to the ball.

The ball was at seven-thirty, quite early, thought Igor, reading the invitation card. It is to be held at the prestigious hall of Chateau de Versailles, at *The Grand Trianon's Cotelle Gallery*, which been built for *Marie Antoinette*. 'It is one of the palace's prestigious estates,' he told Maria. 'Many important receptions take place there. But the place is not that important, it is the people who are going to revive the place - am I not right?'

'Well you've a point!'

Hrant seeing his mother so majestic and royal in a very strong royal blue taffeta dress was moved. The dress had been made especially for the event.

Maria had developed her own appearance, simple and elegant, by trying to incarnate the relation between her personal reflections and conviction about beauty. She had proved through experience that the body, and the nature of one's personality, would eventually express the inner mood, indulging to the person's choice. The image projected reflects the wearer's character and personality. In her situation for that special evening, she wanted to express beauty and class, leaving aside the Swiss simplicity, to show she was the wife of an Armenian aristocrat. The pearl and diamond necklace adorning her abundant breast was making her even truer than anything authentic. She was also wearing the old tiara of the family- with real pearls, rubies and diamonds - that many of the ancestral women in the family had worn hundreds of years back. A matching pearl and diamond gold bracelet, with a rosette centrepiece, enriched the overall impression of aristocratic opulence. The jewellery had been designed by Armenian orfèvers of their times. Maria also opted to wear for the occasion the Bagratuni ring, a big diamond incrusted with rubies and small old cut baguettes, which signed the breath-taking apparition of the royal entity.

Igor and Hrant had almost the same sophisticated look, both being modern royals, each sporting suits of the latest cut. A black frock worn by Igor and a grey frock suit with stripes on the side was the choice of Hrant for that gala evening.

Versailles looked majestic. From the main entrance, one could admire the sublime 17th century architecture. The entire palace was bathed in light. The weather was warm, with a barely perceptible breeze stirring the royal flags. It conferred a peaceful feeling of bathing in eternity. The magnificent picture of Trianon's garden offered a mood of drowsiness through its imbedded scents, emitted by the colourful efflorescent flowers. These were not just any flowers, they were an exclusive floral tribute to emphasise the palace's magniloquent garden. Gushing water was springing out of huge fountains graced by the presence of marble statues of naked Venuses and Apollo. Undeniably, the guests were hugely impressed by the sheer magnificence and aura of the tasteful surroundings. The old palace, majestic and impressive, was standing there, saluting the Bagratuni family, acknowledging their past and present royal appurtenance, to bolster, brace, and sustain their aristocratic reality.

They were by far the most prestigious guests of the palace that evening. They were the only 'crowned' personages in the five hundred prestigious visitors. Among the many eminent guests there were French ministers, and the ambassadors of the Republic of Armenia, Switzerland, and of Russia, together with stars of the world of art and sciences.

The Bagratunis, of course, were the talk of the society. Everybody was eager to meet this outstanding and celebrated aristocratic family, conspicuous and distinguished, as they were, the symbol of the past at the threshold of the 21st century, representing the remnants of the glorious past of the Armenian people. Indeed, they were a prestige to hail, a status to admit, an esteem to carry out. These families, along with their courageous peoples, had steadfastly fought for so many hundreds of years, facing with pride and integrity their unequal struggle of survival. They had gone through so many sacrifices, given away so many of their lands, their riches, to be able to keep their ancestry, lineage and the well-being of their subjects and their homeland. They were the symbol of aspiration; their subjects had their hearts set on their courage. They were confident and had trust first in their God and then in their lords and leaders.

The bitter reality of a complex geographical situation, along with xenophobic, discriminative neighbours, had held back the prosperous growth of their subjects. Their history was full of treachery, unrest and wars. They were obliged to migrate, always looking, with expediency and pragmatism, for a safe haven in which to restart a circumspect, innocuous stable life in a non-hostile and friendly environment, together with the same compulsion and will, to perpetrate the traditional Armenian life.

Back to the ballroom

Sara was not yet in her place. A special table was reserved for her parents and the Bagratunis. She had the duty of an usher yet to fulfil; to greet and to escort the eminent guests into the ballroom, a delicate task designed by the reception committee.

Hrant met Sara while she was crossing the empty gala ballroom, in that beautiful royal environment of gold and red. They stood there speechless She was so surprised to see him in the empty ballroom.

Hrant made the first step forward towards her, happy and flabbergasted, unable to believe his luck at seeing her. 'So here you are, Sara? Good evening, my love.' Moving closer, he took her elegant and soft hand and kissed it. Then, looking into her eyes, he said, 'I hope I did not startle you.'

No, no,' she murmured.

'You are so elegant and lovely tonight. You look like a Dame of Napoleon's time. In one word the most beautiful girl I have ever met.'

She blushed. She felt light and happy, the compliments of Hrant made her feel confident and self-assured. If only he knew the trouble she had gone to choosing her apparel. She had visited all the best boutiques in Paris. Needless to say, Anna and Sophia had helped her. Their unanimous choice was for a pale blue, long dress, subtly adorned with silver lace, and pinned with diamonds and pearls. The dress, which was shimmering under the strong light of the reception room, was accentuating to the full, her sexy and feminine silhouette.

Silk organza raiment, simple and elegant; with a long trail giving the dress a more exquisite and majestic look. The tag of her dress bore the name of Pierre Balmain, a renowned designer at the service of women for so many decades, to enhance their feminine attire. Of course, he wanted to bolster and brace their desire to seduce and induce different messages, to mirror their personalities. Initially, beauty is relevant to a woman's attire, reflecting the images of simplicity, sexiness, elegance, or sophistication.

Sara wanted so much to please Hrant. To her, no one else counted. She'd never felt this warmth towards anyone before, only for her prince. Now here she was, standing here and savouring his adoring gaze. It wasn't how she had dreamt and fantasised about this momentous encounter; Hrant's impatience and daring character had taken her by surprise!

He said, 'Sara I know you are busy, but once you are ready, I will have the first dance with you. Tonight is our night. I will wait for you, Sara.' He paused, struggling for the right words. 'Did you meet my mother and father?'

'No, Hrant. As you can see, I was giving last instructions to the waiters about the flower arrangements and other small details. I must have missed them at the entrance door.'

'Well, let me take you to them.' This said, he approached Sara, took her gently by the arm, and she then strolled at his side, gracious and enthralled, the trail of her gorgeous dress, soft and light, dancing behind her feet.

They were both now marching towards the cocktail lounge, like two lovebirds flying off from the fictitious lands of *One-thousand-and-one nights*, the fairy tail. As Hrant looked around to locate his parents, some women jumped on him, saying 'Oh, your highness, at last we can meet you! We were looking for you!'

Hrant was detached from Sara as elegant women of all ages surrounded him. Once his name was mentioned aloud, most of the guests turned towards him. His parents, seeing Hrant in the small crowd, crossed the room intending to rescue him from his fans. Sara had no chance to say hello to prince Igor and Her Highness Maria Schultess. The crowd around them was so dense, keeping her at a distance. Hrant's parents are so comely and elegant was Sara's reflection, seeing them amid the crowd of curious people. And at that moment her heart filled with pride, knowing she was in love with their son.

Some of the organisers dragged Sara away from the melee. Her admirers were mostly young men who, taking advantage of the situation, driven by her attractiveness, were bringing into play all kind of pretexts, trying to attract and hold her attention, with a train of trivial last minute questions.

The ballroom gradually was filling up. The special guests and VIPs had their tables set on the highest corner of the royal room. The orchestra was playing all kind of soft music to brighten the mood. However, the sight of their daughter's empty chair disappointed Mihran and Sophia. Sara's excusable absence was partly due, of course, to her commitment to assisting with the final arrangements.

The president of the organisation gave a welcoming speech to the guests and wished them a most enjoyable evening. Then she called Prince Bagratuni to say a few words.

Igor was given a standing ovation. It was a moment of exaltation and pride; never before had most of those present had an opportunity to salute a royal family. It was fabulous as some of the guest were shouting in delight.

The prince was clearly moved by the ovation. As he looked around he felt very emotional, and for a moment he stayed speechless, bowing to the guests in all modesty and majesty. He then delivered his speech with sincerity and authority. He told them how proud he felt, and how touched he was by the courage and loyalty of his fellow Armenians, and he spoke of his gratitude to the French people for the love and attention they were showing to his family. He made a solemn promise to continue his sacred duty and philanthropic efforts to keep high and bright the love and faith he had for his people, aware of the many difficulties his people had suffered through the centuries. Fortunately the enemies of yesterday are the friends of today, and the love and care of his family for his nation is as strong as ever. 'Of course,' he had told them, 'we no longer own palaces or regiments of gallant horsemen (laughter and applause followed this) to defend our cause beside big nations. We are living new realities, new world order. The twenty-first century is bathing in new ideologies and new social concepts. It is apprehended through democratic attitudes; henceforth we need to play our role with intelligence and moderation. Modern ideologies are full of new concepts to be understood, but most important is our future contribution in this world of nations. We cannot forget what have we achieved in the past, but we must now explore our current capacities, examine who we are and what are our aspirations. Our most ardent desire, of course, and I am talking in the name of my people, is to enjoy prosperity and peace in our regions. All respect to the countries that have welcomed us as equals and accorded us citizenship. The kind people of these nations have accepted us as brothers and sisters, whilst we, in return, have contributed with hard work and respect to the welfare of those states. Armenians have been very creative and diligent ethnical groups, peaceful and generous, full of compulsion abiding and assimilating, thus bringing its undeniable contribution all through the centuries to the culture, science, astrology, economical, financial and social standing of today. Now I would like to introduce to you my wonderful family.'

He turned to his wife. 'Maria Bagratuni Schulthess is my loving spouse.' Then he gestured toward Hrant. 'And this is my son Hrant, your future prince, who also caries the name of a prominent Armenian sbarabed and prince. He carries also the name of a very eminent intellectual, a man of conviction and courage, our late journalist Hrant Dink, who died for his belief, for having daringly and openly dismissing the Turkish government's denial of the Armenian Genocide, the first genocide of the 20th century.' This was received with loud applause. Then, changing the subject, he went on: 'Unfortunately, our daughter Isabelle is not here tonight.

She would have loved to share this occasion with us, of course - but she is away on an extended trip with her husband Raffi, and could not take part of this wonderful gala. She asked me to pass on her affection and best of thoughts.'

This prompted another round of prolonged applause, everyone getting very emotional in the presence of this respectful eminent family.

'I thank you, all,' Igor said.

As he returned to his table all the guests stood up and continued to applaud, crying out, 'Hail our prince! Long live our prince and his wife Maria!' So Igor time and time again turned his head to thank them for their applause.

The guests had an immense feeling of compassion and respect, towards these people virtually stepping out of history, and were more then ever ready to embrace them as their devout leaders, the proud voice of the past echoing in the annals of the new Millennium, under a new pact, a newfangled synergy.

Igor turned his attention to his devoted family; it was the look of a father, filled with solicitude and pride. Once he sat down, words of warmth and admiration flew from many tables, there was a palpable aura of happiness.

Suddenly a very elegant lady from an adjacent table came over to Igor and asked if he would like to open the ball. Igor was little tired, effectively he asked for a few minutes of rest, before undertaking this unexpected task the president was asking him to perform. He looked at Hrant, whose thoughts were elsewhere; his gaze directed towards the ballroom floor. He was anxious about not seeing Sara, who had not yet come to greet them. Even though he was smiling and very politely returning all the greetings of charm and admiration being lavished upon him, he was suffering again in his inner self, thinking that maybe Sara was with some other attractive gentleman, one of those who were buzzing around her like a wasps on a cream cake.

Igor nodded to Hrant to say you are next on the list. 'I will go first, then you follow my steps.'

Hrant was not happy. His father seemed not to understand that there was no way to start his first dance without Sara. He had given her his word of honour. He wanted to open the ball with her, to show to his fellow patriots that she is the woman who had stolen his heart.

The orchestra started a Viennese Valse of Johannes Strauss.

Igor rose to his feet. He straightened his jacket and with a polite bow to his princess, asked her for the opening dance of the ball.

Maria did not hesitate and in a very feminine manner she accepted the hand of her husband. Hrant helped her with the chair. They walked sauntering, betrothed to each other up until the dancing floor.

The orchestra managed another valse: The Blue Danube. Igor and Maria where dancing like professionals. The couple was following the rhythm of the music and melting in its vibration. It was a wonderful sight; no one dared to derange the show. The royal couple remained there, dancing in wide circles, agile and professional. Maria made a breathtaking picture; she was so feminine and royal in her glittering attire. Hrant was moved, seeing his wonderful parents so young at heart and so much in love.

At last, Sara was on the scene. With slow pace, she approached the VIP guest's table and took her place. She saluted each one, as all the men stood up to greet her. Hrant was the last. He helped her to her place but said nothing.

The second valse was coming to end when Hrant met his father's gaze. He grasped the cue, so he stood up and walked two seats down, to Sara's. His heart was melting at the idea that he was going to hold her waist in his arms and feel her heartbeats.

Sara stood up, bright and glittering. Now all eyes were focusing on the couple. Murmurs of appreciation filled the room.

Sara walked behind Hrant. Just as she had the first time - an eternity had elapsed since that momentous encounter - she felt as if she was not walking, she was sliding lightly, filled with delight. She met the eyes of her parents, they were reflecting the proud and happy parent's stare, fixing their eyes on their child, their daughter. It was a wondrous moment in time, full of bliss and immeasurable pride.

People started to applaud out of emotion. They were seeing for the first time an Armenian prince dancing with a very elegant young woman, most probably a member of another royal family! They were now on the dance floor. Igor and Maria made some final turns, and then vacated the floor, leaving Hrant and Sara charming the guests with their young and flexible dancing steps.

After the first valse was over, couples taking their courage in hand, came to join their prominent honourable guest. Hrant was an excellent dancer. He had this in his genes. His father was as good as he was at his age, even today! Sara did not have much to do. Her musical ear was helping her with the steps. Being light and flexible, she was melting in the arms of Hrant, who was making big rondos, clutching her to his chest, tightly holding her by her waist. Sara was like a cotton poupée, so soft and pliant, attuned to Hrant's movements, meanwhile letting her trail dancing like a wave behind her back, thus adding more majesty to the picturesque display.

They eventually returned to their seats. Compliments and kind words were flowing from every table. Hrant had to invite some of the other young women to the dancing floor, as the protocol and good manners would require. Meanwhile he noticed that Sara was dancing too, with a very elegant and good looking young man. He was concerned, as she seemed to be very relaxed with this young man, who was leading her in huge circles, she letting her body be carried by him, to a point that he was almost bearing the whole weight of her body. Hrant began to feel wary, watchful and anxious even, a feeling of resentment was choking his chest. He was not normally over possessive. Initially, he was surprised by his own reaction and attitude. But watching them again, his concern towards that complete stranger grew!

Who was this man? While he was trying to approach the couple, Sara and Christian left the dancing floor and walked towards a nearby table. At their approach, a very imposing, elderly couple stood up and hugged Sara in a very cheerful and friendly way. As for the man, he bowed to kiss Sara's hand.

Hrant was no longer interested in the dance, nor in the young woman he was dancing with. As soon as the music stopped, he thanked the lady swiftly, and in a fraction of a second, took the same route as Sara had walked with Christian. As he approached their table, the group was still busy talking to Sara. He interrupted their conversation with, 'Sara my darling, there you are. You promised this dance to me.'

Sara turned her head to grab Hrant's arm, and in a soft and sweet voice she said, 'I am here to welcome my best friends. To my great delight they accepted my invitation to tonight's gala ball.' She released Hrant's arm, then started the introductions: 'Hrant, this is Mr and Mrs Cousteau, the parents of my classmate Christian. 'Christian, this is Hrant.'

Christian took a step backward, turned to face Hrant, then with due reverence shook his hand, saying, 'My pleasure, your royal highness.'

Hrant responded with, 'I'm delighted to meet a friend of Sara, I have heard so much about you.'

At this, Christian felt a little embarrassed. After glancing at Sara, he smiled nervously and said, 'I hope they were deserving, suitable comments.'

This time looking to Sara, Hrant replied, 'they were honest remarks, witnessing and evaluating your year-long lasting friendship, isn't that so, Sara?'

Sara was blushing, She felt uneasy inside, seeing these two men were having a challenging exchange. She was attending a direct embroilment, a war of words, defying each other in the most arrogant yet graceful manner. Christian was growing more and more ill at ease, almost constrained, unlike Hrant, who was remaining composed, surer then ever, knowing how to express his feelings with the right words. He always knew how to juggle his impressions with suppleness, Sara thought, how to be wordy without hurting, having the capacity to balance his emotions with the fitted statement and manners.

Turning back to Christian's parents, Hrant awarded them a few kind words, by welcoming them again, and wishing them an enjoyable evening, mostly adding his appreciation in the name of the organisation and the committee for their endeavour by having contributed to their cause. Christian's mother was under his spell. People from all around were now watching this small group. He was being interrupted many times, but always responding with a smile, and getting on with the cordial presentation, making the acquaintance of Christian and his parents. Hrant had become more intrigued, full of interest, having met them. This encounter was his first surprise of the evening. Effectively it was the first obstacle of the evening, the black shadow that came into the ideal picture, to deter from its perfection, reminding one that nothing is perfect enough to defy the balance of cosmic power, that happiness is an illusion of a moment, to be lived and grabbed! Perfection is only God!

Challenge in his head, wariness in his heart, Hrant walked to his table followed by Sara. They exchanged no words. Hrant looked at Sara as if to say, this was a surprise! You never mentioned them, did you? You were forming a very good couple with Christian!

Several minutes elapsed. They were both sitting there, surrounded by merry people. Hrant, deep in thought, realised he had behaved in a very emotional way, acting in an over protective way. He had undermined Sara's feelings and happy mood, especially by acting so in front of a very inquisitive crowd. The ballroom was buzzing now: music, dancing, raised conversations. He turned his gaze to Sara, who was sitting there, lonely, disappointed, hurt in her woman ego, detached from all other guests. She was no longer merry, and her smile was being replaced by intense frowns, which displaced her usual charming aura. She was in her jumbled inner world, not knowing what to do. For the first time she was encountering Hrant's excessive emotion, not to say jealous state. She and Christian had been friends for a decade; however, she had never encouraged his advances. She always looked upon him as her best friend. She was keen on him indeed, but on a different level. Obviously, his parents considered her as a very close friend of the family, and she felt very close to them too, but never dreamt of becoming their daughter. She was confused, and did not feel the need to justify her behaviour on the dance floor. Yes, maybe she felt well in the arms of Christian; that was undeniably true. But it was merely a brief moment feeling nostalgic of her school circle, feeling young and worry-free, joyful like in her schooldays. If Hrant could not appreciate that difference, accepting to see her happy with others, it was his problem. He had to learn, to see her relax with others, the way she would do regarding his dealings, confronting such difficulties and making some concessions, and not be conceited. He had to learn to accept her to be herself, not to feel pressured, to live a life of constant watchfulness. They must share mutual confidence to each other, and build real trust. Temptation is everywhere in one form or another, always, for everyone. If there is no mutual respect and honest and strong love, then nothing can be fulfilling or long lasting. No oaths can be believed, nor love respected.

From time to time they were exchanging nervous looks, not knowing who was to undertake the first step.

Hrant at last decided to stand up. It was for him to earn back Sara's broken heart. Acknowledging in all sincerity that he had to change his attitude, and try to make some concessions in the future, to keep up with the facets of love in its hidden shades. He approached Sara's chair and without calling her name, he reached out and took her hand, while searching the beautiful eyes of his fairytale princess. His heart melted at her honest look, her expression wordlessly telling him: My darling, Christian is only a doting friend. You are my only true love!

They sat side by side, maintaining their shared silence. There was no longer a need to speak; their hearts were as one. There was a clear understanding of unspoken fondness. They were of different planets and born under different stars. One was bind to Mars the other to

Venus! Their destiny was to bring together these two poles apart cosmic elements.

Before the guests would come out to see "Versailles Water Night," the orchestra played an Armenian folk dance, inviting all to join in. The organisers had to take the initiative to lead the dance. Of course, in the beginning, not many responded to the invitation, but once Hrant stood up and took Sara's hand, leading her towards the dance floor, couples of all ages, encouraged by their example, strode to follow them on to the floor. There, they were dancing to an Armenian old folk tune in all tempos.

Hrant and Sara were proficient in Armenian Folk dance. They were ardently showing their foreign guests how to bend their legs. One two three jeté, the knee bent, then straighten the legs up, then pull back, and make a turn with your feet on the floor, next make a small jeté on the other side. It was easy and did not matter how well they were dancing. What mattered was that they were taking part with humour and goodwill, shaking and jumping, and harmoniously following the vibration and the tonality of the folk music. Armenians are grateful to the genius of composer 'Komitas Vartabed' who, at the beginning of the 20th century, had the brilliant idea of collecting songs from different villages, and from scattered Armenian cities, then rearranging them in their final theme. Hundreds of years old songs played today in the revised versions. Those were the token songs, the spirit of the Armenian folk, which were sung and danced to by its people, in both their sad and happy moments.

Sara, Sophia and Maria, along with many other ladies, took part in the folk dancing, dragging with them foreign guests, unfamiliar with the dance and its alien tune. They were all dancing and trying to imitate the steps of the group's leader, who had a special name in Armenian: *Tamadaan.*

The ladies on the dance floor were having a slight problem. The weight of their long trails was preventing their legs from moving freely and thus dancing properly and spontaneously. They were trying their best to manage their long skirts, very tactfully and elegantly, hoping to avoid them being trampled on by the other lively dancers, full in the rhythm of the tempo. But Maria could not escape the unthinkable; she was in trouble with a young guy, who had inadvertently trod on the tail of her dress, tearing off the black lace sawn on the border of the trail. It was now hanging down awkwardly. The energetic young dancer, through the pressure of his strong footstep, had ripped off the soft material. Maria responded with a laugh, asking the boy not to break his rhythm, the cadence of the dance. 'Go ahead, my son, don't stop. It's okay, that's not a big deal, nothing to worry about. I can fix it tomorrow.' And the boy smiled graciously and went to hold the hand of one of the dancers, not detaching his eyes from that wonderful lady.

Sweat was running from Hrant's body. He was thrilled; he stopped for a moment to watch the crowd around him. People young at heart were whole-heartedly taking part in the dance. He was calling for an ovation. Guests were under the spell of the Armenian music. A ravishing moment, holding the hand of his future mother-in-law in his right hand, and with his prospective father-in-law on the left, he tried to lead them, making more circles, rejoicing and hailing the moment. Tables were almost empty now everybody was on the floor. The mood was joyous; there was laughter everywhere. By God, what a success!

Close to midnight all of the guests had the luck to attend the awesome spectacle of 'Versailles Big Water Nightly' - a special programme offered by the organisers. Versailles by night accompanied by music and fireworks. It was a moment to remember, an event to fill one's heart with wonder and ecstasy.

Versailles was discrete when it dealt with glamour and romance. Every corner of its extensive estate, love and pretty intrigues had been denoted, an indication of its glorious past. Secret love affairs were sung, poems were written by eminent writers and poets like *Guillaume Appolinaire, Voltaire, Montesquieu* and many others, alluding, and suggesting on passion, power, wars and intrigues, connotations that lived in the gardens of the walls of the palace. The architects like *Francois Boucher* and *Marie de Laurencine* were inspired through the powerful mistresses of the palace.

The spirit of Marquise de *Pompadour*, the mistress of Louis XV, soaring through the statues of the *Trianon Petit Palais*, specially built for her by the king. The Marquise was the guardian, being the Patron of Arts and Literature, creator of the rococo manner of design; her spirit had never let down the Versailles, bondage of ardour and passion being inscribed on every stone.

The lovers of Versailles were the yearning spectres of aspiration, drawn to lust, to excessive emotional upheavals. Today they were the phantoms, the poltergeists full of vehement emotions, craving of amorous appetite, mixed with intrigue and malice, reckoning with pulping hearts. They had the innate nature to savour, exalt, while enjoying the game of love, of forbidden dangerous lust, relishing in delight the wide skirts of their lovers.

There was a crowd of leprechauns and elves that night. They were all there, the spectre of the conjured up apparition of those lovers, mistresses of noblemen and commoners, soaring along with the wraith of their queen of heart, Marie Antoinette and her lover *Hans Axel Fersen*. They were all enchanted, to celebrate a pure and earnest love of a young couple of another century, of newer times. He was a prince, the historic figure, and she a commoner, the maiden of the new era, kneeling side by side, heart in heart to celebrate the moment, the illusion of a split second.

Hrant and Sara declared their love and eternal bondage to each other, solemnly filled with affection and rapture. They were bound to tender passion, a warm feeling of esteem and admiration for each other. These lovebirds, winsome and charming, were engaging their lives for a committed future. Destiny had chosen the walls of Versailles, and a joyful event of laughter and merriment, to endorse the pact of their union. Their amorousness was a joy for all these floating phantoms; these spirits were their silent witnesses, to work their spell and incantation. Each scent, each music note, was an invocation of their concern and contentment, for this vehement attractive pair.

Sara and Hrant had fused in love, fond of each other filled with tender affectionate amour. As for the future, it had to pave the way and make life wonderful for this new promising, congenial couple. Indeed the diversity of the spectacle was a sublimation of sight. Hand in hand, like a real couple, they were for the first time, able to share a modest degree of intimacy. Hrant held her to his chest. Unexplained sensational emotions wrestled in Sara's innermost being. Moreover, for the first time, she felt Hrant's heartbeats and felt so utterly content in his company, so close to his soul. All this was so new to her, losing her heart to someone, to be drawn so intensely, and being inflamed, delightfully to that extend!

They were trying to hide themselves from curious eyes by choosing the dark and romantic areas of the gardens. These were magical moments for them both. A strong game of light and music was indulging and igniting all their five senses, delightful and engaging, paving the way to their new happiness. They were both sweating under the pressure of their sweet feelings. They hardly spoke; only some sweet exclamations being heard, sounds that were being echoed through their hearts. The waters were scintillating under the reflection of light, as if the stars had fallen into the fountains. It was a pure moment of transparency. In that electrical moment, everything was possible. The past was mingling with the reality of the present, history repeating itself at the threshold of the 21st century.

The aftermath of the ball

Both parents promised to meet before leaving for Switzerland. Hrant was to stay a few more days at Sara's request. She dearly wanted to organise some more outings, to satiate the desire of an enamoured woman! The day following the ball was like a bolt out of the blue. People who were not present in the reception soon learned of the couple's obvious affection for each other. The Bagratuni family was on the scene - always a sure draw for the attention of the international media.

Captured in the spotlight of publicity, neither Sara nor Hrant could hide their relationship. Switzerland was their ideal refuge to stay away from curious rumourmongers. Indeed Swiss people were educated, to be discrete and to recognize and esteem the privacy of their eminent visitors: crown heads, actors, and famous sport figures, and let them enjoy their country like simple folks at ease, transparent, respecting their freedom, to go around without being invaded by the look or to come within reach of curious people! They tried to make the most of these few days they had together, seeing some revues; taking long walks and shopping in the boutiques of *Champs Elise*, visiting *Le Louvre Mont Martre* with all its street painters and cafés. Their youth, joie de vivre and dynamism were making their sojourn even more remarkable.

Hrant met Sara at the university's entrance. There was a crowd of prominent young women and men, the future denominators of their society, a new age group of contemporaries – students who had to prove themselves in different ways. Their aspiration for tomorrow and their worry about so many subjects, retrieving in differed ways to the previous generation.

Before parting, Sara expressed the full depth of her feelings to Hrant. He felt his blood boiling, 'I too had the best moments of my life,' he replied. 'All the pleasure and happiness was mine, my darling, you are my tender passion and future backbone.' He embraced her tightly. 'Do not forget my precious angel that the best is yet to come.'

'Is that a royal promise, my darling?'

As an answer, Sara received the warmest kiss a man in love could ever bestow.

Noah and Ararat; myth and reality

Both sets of parents met the day after the ball. During the dinner they had invoked the fondness that their children were having towards each other, and that attachment made their ties stronger. They were full of good wishes and long lasting affability and fulfilment of desire for their children. Both sets of parents were overjoyed and equally delighted by this union. They drank to the happiness of their children, enjoying the cherished moment, making promises to meet every now and then, either in Switzerland or France. They even planned to take a trip to Armenia together, to encounter Ararat.

Mihran was very excited by the prospect of a visit to Armenia. He said, 'I miss Ararat, our ancestral mountain. I am getting on in years now, and I think it is time for Sophia and me to give our "venerated mountain" a warm visit.

Igor frowned, clearly bemused. 'How can that be? You have never been there, Mihran.'

'I have been to Armenia many times, but for so many reasons I had postponed my visit to Ararat. I did admire him though, from the Yerevan border. It is so majestic and inspiring, watchful over our lands. Indeed, it is the symbol of pride to the Armenians all over the world. Actually, we identify our origins through its powerful and eternal presence. In fact, at 5400 metres it is the fifth highest mountain in the world. I have never climbed it, of course, but alpinists say its summit is covered with a crown of snow all year round. Sadly, today it is in Turkish hands.' After pausing for breath, he went on, 'did you know that the Greek savant *Xenophon* had been in Armenia in 401 BC in *Anabas*? If we go back to tradition, the region of Ararat, also called the Garden of Eden, due to many ancient scriptures, and that in Hebrew it means Armenia.'

'It's the oldest region, isn't it?'

'According to the story of Noah, from the Bible, Ararat was the mountain on which his boat, with its animal kingdom aboard, rested to escape the big flood. With all these inscriptions, one can conclude that the territory of the Armenian plateau was the cradle of the ancient civilisation. Armenians, for hundred of years, lived in the region of its plateau and built many cities around its fertile lands.'

This time Igor took the lead of the subject: 'Armenians of the Ararat region, as I am sure you know, my dear Mihran, have very characteristic traits. They are strong and tall, fair complexioned, and excellent horse riders. On my frequent visits to the area, I met some Armenians living in the vicinity. I was told about their trouble dealing with the region's harsh weather, its long winter climate, and an arid summer to confront after the cold weather.'

'Were there Armenians still living there?' asked Mihran, flabbergasted.

'Yes, I was surprised too, my dear Mihran. I had to ask around to find some specimen. However, they mostly spoke Turkish, and a special dialect peculiar to the area. It remains very rural, and very old-fashioned attire is still the order of the day there. They do not disclose their identity, unless they are sure of the stranger they are dealing with.'

'Really? How amazing!' gasped Mihran.

'I too am surprised,' uttered Sophia, who was listening intently, 'since we all know that they were driven out of the plateau around the beginning of the 20th century!'

'Well yes, my dear Sophia, but some, not having the resources to start a new life, had to remain there. Some migrated from Crimea or Georgia after the communist era, to embrace what kind of living, accepting what kind of life?

'Actually,' (continues Igor with the same enthusiasm) alluding the subject of Lake Van and Ararat regions, 'I was invited to a lecture by an eminent Armenian scholar, Ara Sarafian, a historian and the director of the *Gomidas Institute* in London. His lecture was on "Disappearing Armenian Monasteries in Turkey". He expressed the need to preserve the traditional history of the Armenians in Turkish territory. According to Ara Sarafian, continuous maintenance is essential in preventing the complete destruction of the few remaining monasteries in the region of Lake Van, and it is the responsibility of Armenians to keep Armenian history alive. Well, we all agree that he has a point, don't we? We must all do our best to contribute towards that end, to attract the attention of our people and the Turkish government's help.'

'Yes indeed,' Sophia said earnestly.

'Mihran,' Igor said, changing the subject, 'did you appreciate the parallel of these two mountains. It is so funny.'

'I'm not sure what you mean?'

'Well for example, Ararat is the highest mountain in its region, and the Alps chain, with Monte Rosa as its highest peak of 4634 metres, the highest in Switzerland, and Mont Blanc Massif of 4808 metres is the highest in France. The people living around their plateau also have rather strong and harsh features. Candid and laborious rural inhabitants populate both mountains. They are both striking mountains full of historical blueprints.'

'Why, yes,' said Mihran, 'I see what you mean.'

Igor nodded and directed his gaze at Maria. 'Another shared feature is the Edelweiss flower. These rare flowers blooming on the mountains of the Alps are becoming the pride of the Swiss and Austrian people. We also have Edelweiss on the Ararat Mountain. Did you know about that, my Swiss lady?' he asked with a teasing smile.

'To be honest Igor,' came Maria's warm and feminine reply. 'I did not know about Edelweiss on Ararat. I am sure there are many other species there too, just like on the Alps. Yes, I have heard about important herbs growing on its bosom – esoteric, elixir, medicinal herbs, nourished in its pure soil and pollution free sunny weather. I am looking forward to seeing all these beauty soon, to enhance my footprint on this majestic landscape. I am sure of one thing: it will heighten my perspective by taking me close to cosmic space. We will be watching for the first time, shining across its blue immaculate sky, elevated to the realms of its cosmic curtain, where are hidden its most shiny stars, like the watchful eyes of our ancestors! As our eminent historian, Mr Sarafian, has urged us, *we must enliven our consciousness towards that end, to keep alive our historical ancestral Armenia!*'

They were thrilled and enthusiastic like schoolmates preparing the school's yearly trip. They were happy people, engulfing the moment's cherished events in simplicity and modesty. They were already fulfilled and satisfied with the idea, and if that scheme did not fulfil its promise, they were still winners since they already had enjoyed the moment's inspiration. This was the attitude of the Armenian genetically implemented; some did not even question their attitude towards the given of their character. Faithful to their nature, they just lived the moment's token, since they knew "domani" would never come!

The farewell

Igor was very emotional on the day of their departure. He felt he was leaving a brother behind him. In Switzerland he had few friends with this degree of closeness and warmth. They were birds of the same feather; their deep understanding about many matters such as family bonding, care and moral issues, were the same. They had suffered and struggled with the same problems having to do with identity, integration and dwelling - questions of huge scale. They both had to fight for their imminent rights, to raise their children in the realities of both the present and their inherited past, a history full of pride, defiance, and compulsion.

The reverberation of an age-long friendship

Sara had to return to her studies. She came upon her best friend, Juliet, who was anxious not to have had her company around the campus for a while. Juliet and Sara were best friends, since their childhood. They always shared their deep secrets and talked on many subjects. Therefore it was natural for Sara to share her heart's sweet secret, informing her about Hrant.

On hearing the details of her friend's encounter with a prince, Juliet's expressions changed. Her green eyes got bigger, and her cheeks grew pink with excitement. Sara smiled on seeing her friend's reaction. She continued without pause, this time with more passion in her voice. 'We both are so much attracted to each other, physically and spiritually. I love him, my young and handsome prince. I love him as I have never loved anyone before, that much you know, Juliet, don't you?'

Juliet nodded 'Yes of course, Sara, I have never seen you so emotional, so passionate until this day.'

'I love him, Juliet, from the bottom of my heart and soul, my whole being trembles when I think of him. He bears all the characteristics of his heritage. He is a responsible person, incredibly mature for his age. He likes to help people, always being considerate and kind at heart, full of understanding and patience. He is such a well-balanced guy. Even though I feel sometimes that he is detached and composed, but I know deep inside, he is the warmest and most compassionate person. For example, at the ball he did not hesitate to encourage his fellow participants to dance an Armenian folk dance at the heart of Versailles Palace. Somebody else with his title would act in a condescending manner and snub the public; all just the opposite.'

'Well,' goes Juliet, 'men in general do not perceive and observe as we women do, and if he is an engaged boy, full of activity for the Armenian cause, it means you have to be patient with your relationship!'

Sara gave a pompous grimace, and Juliet went on: 'Especially if he is not around. He is living in Switzerland, isn't he?' But you will see each other from time to time, and so you will miss each other many times!'

This time Sara, in a defensive tone, replied, 'Of course I will be patient, Juliet, even though it will be so hard on me. I have to make some concessions, a solemn promise to wait for him, as long as is necessary to maintain our caring relationship. I know that it is not easy to be an Armenian prince, just the same way as it is for me or any Armenian commoner, only more so. To impose your title or your origin is somehow not evident, especially when people do not know about your history, and are initially full of prejudice, often derisive and cynical, jumping to unfounded conclusions.

'But I have never treated you in that way, Sara - you are my dear friend and I love you,' countered Juliet, a little bit hurt by her friend's indirect attack. 'I consider you as French as I am.'

'Well of course, Juliet, that's exactly what I want to point out,' explained Sara, 'especially since for years all my friends, from here or afar, see my French side and know very little about me and my family. That is exactly what I want to point out.'

'But I know that you are an Armenian,' replied Juliet, with some emotion, shaken physically. 'Only I did not know that you were this much emotionally involved to your origin.'

'Of course I am, Juliet, everybody is attached to and proud of his or her origin. Aren't you proud of being French? Don't you learn about the history of your glorious past? Not to undermine the pride you have to own a big emperor like Napoleon Bonaparte in your national inheritance, a man who was able to make all of Europe tremble. You boast of their legacy, you are proud of all the victories and the triumphs, and you do not hesitate to recall their defeats too, which makes of France an outstanding nation, a country, which learns from his past glories and mistakes. Undoubtedly you love your literature, your writers and philosophers such as *Jean Jacque Rousseau, Lamartine, Gustave Flobert, Alexander Dumas, Victor Hugo, Jean Paul Sartre,* to name only a few. You are proud of their heritage, the tradition and the richness they bestowed.

'Yes, you are right,' Juliet hurriedly agreed, trying to calm Sara, who was keyed up. 'But this does not make me, or give me the right to think that I am a better or more superior person than you!'

'Ha,' said Sara 'but some people do take advantage of this issue. The French are known to be chauvinistic people, which is why, maybe, we Armenian students and Armenians in general have to work harder than others. Accepting criticism is profoundly rooted in all of us. Deep inside, wanting to prove ourselves, by braving our ambitions as being good, without being ostentatious. We have to be more motivated than most to succeed in our endeavours. Today we are able to aspire to higher education and creativity, thanks to the countries we are living in. We are lucky to flourish in a peaceful environment and to enjoy the facilities available to our generation. We are much luckier than our previous generation, who could not enjoy this liberty and peace and all the advantages now at hand. The late French director *Ashod Malakian*, in his film "Mayrig" pointed out this problem clearly. But with all of this said, I am proud that I belong and am well assimilated to a big nation like France, which is the cradle of so many ethnic groups. So many minorities find their peaceful haven under her beautiful sky.'

Sara paused for emphasis, then went on, 'My dearest Juliet, I would like to underline the fact that for centuries our nation was being subdued by migration and deportation; by searching for a safe haven, longing for the ideal country. They all went on dreaming of the land of their cherished memory, not to tend to forgetfulness. Trying to teach their children from where they are coming, who they are and what are their aspirations and longings! We are a peaceful and cultivated nation, enduring and braving all kind of difficulties. We express and show respect and keenness to the countries where we were born and raised. Discriminative attitudes by ignorant people created a kind of distress, a wound, and sadness in us. It is not easy to be ignored, to be misunderstood and not totally accepted as individuals trying to appreciate the difference, instead of appointing the disparity. Acknowledge the whereabouts and value the aspiration and the virtue of an Armenian individual, who brought his knowledge, enthusiasm, his savoir-faire, and his driving force and positive stance towards life, and attempt towards integration.'

'Is this why you and Christian could not stay together?'

Sara blushed; she was not expecting this direct question from her friend. She hesitated for some time, then, she raised her head high and said, 'One day a patient of my father, who happened to be Polish, tells him, "Dr. Mihran, I am flattered to meet a good person like you." My father was taken aback by this declaration. "Why are you astounded?" my father asked his patient, "Did an Armenian once hurt your feelings?" The man shook his head and replied, "No, not especially, dear doctor, but the truth is that in Poland I heard that Armenians are rather in unorthodox businesses, especially the ones from the East."

My father very calmly adds: "Well, Mr Igenivitch, there are such groups of individuals in every nation. Armenians are no exception, especially the ones living in environments that are full of different nationalities, and who are the instigators of such organisations. We Armenians have individuals bearing all kind of characteristics, people of all categories: rich and poor, intelligent, less intelligent, knowledgeable, diligent, assiduous, and so many indolent, irresponsible persons. Armenians are more or less conservative and moralist persons, but we also have unfortunately less moralist and materialist people, who want to get rich from one day to the other. Inevitably this kind of connotation won't make them a lesser person, bad or appalling. Nay, not at all. Do you not think that this is the depiction of all nations, notwithstanding big or small? We are not all born from the same parents," he goes on laughing, "but we are derived and flow from the same stream. We came into existence and germinated from the same fields, valleys, and mountains. For 1,700 years we prayed to the same Christian God, we kneeled down to the same enemy, we drank the same bitter drink and shared the same nightmare. Our aspirations and dreams had the same obsession and assess - the fulfilment of a free and peaceful land."

Whereupon the man replied, "I feel very ashamed, Doctor. Today I am learning something new about the Armenian people. I would like to apologise for my quick wording and prejudice, and I am thankful of your explanation."

'So you see, Juliet, why am I so anxious,' Sara said quietly. 'It is merely because of such arrogant, unnecessary, and inconsiderate statements that I am mostly irritated. People do not know much about you, yet they judge you and fear the difference!'

'Yes, I understand what you mean, Sara.'

"I am aware of my identity and I assume fully its discrepancies. Suppose I was born of another origin, believe me, Juliet, I would have defended and accepted its virtue and value as I am doing with my present status - with pride, integrity, and respect.'

'Well now, my dearest Sara, leave aside your national feelings, to come back to your utmost, imminent reality. You should enjoy wholeheartedly this happy event of outstanding encounter, where you met the love of your life. You should treasure every moment of this wonderful new relationship you now have, rather than trouble yourself with those issues. Effectively you should consider your own happiness, which is for the moment more important than any such issues. I am so happy for you Sara, my French–Armenian friend' Juliet added with a sweet smile. 'Not only have you found the man of your heart, but you also have a nobleman of Armenian origin. Congratulations, Sara, try to be happy! I hope I will soon meet your Prince.' Getting closer, Juliet took Sara in her arms and gave her a big, warm hug.

Then Juliet had another direct question for Sara. 'How about Christian?'

Sara smiled, she knew deep in her heart Juliet was boiling for the answer to that question. 'Well, my dear Juliet, Christian is in love with me, I know, and I regret that I am the cause of his misery. There was a time I was attracted to him. Then, we were young and immature. As we mature our interests and desires, our likes and dislikes, are subject to change. I do love Christian, albeit in a different way. He is my friend and I cherish him. We grew up together and his parents considered me part of their family. My feelings and attitude altered towards him the moment I saw Hrant. I was attracted to him, I cannot explain why!' Sara paused, then in a very abstract voice continues, 'All I know is that I was fascinated by him. It was love at first sight. When I first saw him, I knew deep inside that he was the man of my life. We were drawn by the mutual magnetism. Our hearts pierced with the thorns of love.'

'That sounds so romantic, Sara.'

'Yes, we are constantly under love's alluring spell, as if we are constantly being moulded, kneaded through our emotions. By marrying him, I would marry the whole Armenian history. He is the seat of our past and present. With him, space and time have another measure, another reality. When I am with him I feel trapped in my desires, and confined in my illusions. I am taken away in the midst of the blue sky, travelling on the wings of the far away stars, to unknown realms, soaring above in the scintillating galaxies, bathing in their lights. I have a feeling of engulfing the infinite souls of twenty some generations, reincarnating their spirits in a whirlpool of enchantment. I have the sensation that I knew him a long time ago, as of the times of our glorious past, during our **Cilician kingdom**.' The excitement was evident in Sara's voice.

'And Christian? Does he not have many admirable qualities too?'

'Christian is a French man full of present-day history. I do not need that! Already I am living French history with my everyday life. What I need, Juliet is to thrive on our past, prevail in the present, by dealing with gratifying worthwhile issues. To live a future that is full of adventure and white-hot events. This entire quest, these ventures, is possible only with Hrant. I can assist him in his future path; he needs so much a French–Armenian woman, who can contribute to that end. Our exploits might not be easy. It might be full of obstacles, contradictions, difficulties, dealing with the intricate unsolved problems, political ethnical or patrimonies, who are left behind in the hand of alien people. I am ready and solicited to make those concessions and accept the challenges, no matter how timely or how knotted they will be. I have a high esteem, deference, and look with high regard his commitments, while dealing with so many such issues, at such a young age!

'With Christian, my dear Juliet, my life would be so different It would be tranquil, winsome - a life with no contempt, as if inundated with a fountain of French perfumes, spread all over in a décor of laces. France is paved with the best cultural treasures, the most fantastic works of art to admire and be proud of, the literature of famous writers, read by millions. But No! My vocation, Juliet, is elsewhere, my heartbeat is for my Hrant, and with him, I will be embracing all our past treasures, frail or strong, rich or poor, humble and modest. To challenge our past forgotten kingdoms that were demeaned and disdained most of the time, remembered and paid tribute only by its native people.'

'You really are serious about this, aren't you, Sara?'

'I have the sacred duty, my young friend, to enhance all these ambitions with Hrant, even though he is a Swiss-Armenian, albeit, he inclines more to the his Armenian heritage, mostly as of his mission. Hand in hand with my fellow friends, we will bring forth and contrive to awaken the memory of condescending nations - neighbours most of the time - to the fact that we have contributed so much to their welfare. We have assigned and contributed to the civilisation of the world. I want young generations to be acquainted with our past, be aware of our forgotten kingdom of Cilicia to be aware about big generals and kings that ruled and served other countries and their role in the history for so many centuries.'

There was a long silence. Juliet was under the spell of her friend's emotional recounting. Awed by the details, under the spell of her narrative. She was living the magic charm of a love story, and the details of a dearest friend's encounter with the man of her origin.

'If you are apt to live the sensations of love,' resumed Sara, 'Sensations that would make you shiver, waves of feelings that would gobble up your smooth senses.' She took a deep breath. 'It would paw and palpate your innermost feelings, by spreading a kind of fondness that would bring out all the serenity of the moment, until the next experience, until the next encounter. We love each other so much that nothing can come between us. I love him every time more.'

'Oh, so much passion!' cries out Juliet, jumping and smiling in her excitement.

'No it's not only passion, my dear Juliet, it is a lifelong commitment. Moreover, that frightens me sometimes! I am not very close to his mother yet, though. I hope that will come about with time, knowing the love he has for both his parents, especially, his mother, she is Swiss you know, and I don't know yet Swiss character that much!'

Juliet responded with a hearty chuckle. 'Well my dear Sara, it a known fact that mothers-in-law do not like to share their son with the best of women. But I am sure with your subtle and friendly character, you will find the right way to cope with the situation!' Weighing her words carefully, she went on, 'As for Christian, well, you always knew what you wanted; from the time we became friends. Well, you never mentioned to marry someone of your own native origin, and your thesis on the Armenian issue had a big impact on everyone.'

'Well Juliet, I am sure he will find a nice woman to make him happy, someone just like you.'

Juliet's smile was almost a blush. That statement needed some serious contemplation. So instead of voicing a reply, she hugged her friend again, and they parted with a cheery wave.

Part IV

Back to Switzerland

Hrant returned to Zurich by plane. He was a little nervous. That morning the bank had called him; VIP guest from abroad were coming, and his presence was required. He had to rush home to prepare the files, to report the client's exigencies. He had not had enough time to commit the details to memory.

On the plane, the flight attendant offered him a glass of champagne; while indulging his palate, he fixed the bubbles, whose recollection evoked into him a sudden desire to go back to Sara, to his fairytale. The magic of the bubbles took him back to the many happy hours he spent in Paris. He was already nostalgic and regretful not to be with them all: Sara, Mihran, Sophia, and Anna.

He had lived the prime of his life among people whom he cared the most for. He had found the most exquisite Armenian family and friends, not to mention of the most precious Armenian girl. No match found unless between Armenians themselves, he thought, and he smiled at this, thinking of his exaggerated theory and of his Swiss mother! After a quick sigh, Hrant came to a new accepted wisdom, assessing and scrutinizing the givens of the latest coincidence of his life, under a new light. He was solicited to a new condition, aware of the fact that from now on, his heart was to hang about, apt to be more often in France, where lies his heart's yearning. Nevertheless, he had to maintain a pragmatic approach and tackle his obligations to his parents and his business and stay for a while in Zurich.

Father and mother had enjoyed their trip. Mother was the first to pronounce her happiness for having seen Sara together with Hrant. She had told him, 'you make a beautiful couple. Sara has class and charm, and she is also very mature person for her age and incredibly well educated. That is clear to me even though I didn't have the chance to talk with her that often,' she had added with regret in her voice. 'I think Mihran and Sophia can be proud of their daughter.

'You were the talk of the whole Armenian, French and Swiss societies,' Igor said proudly.

'Well,' continued Maria in a more emotional tone, 'it was not altogether that evident that she had to meet a noble gentleman. It's a pity that your father did not want to meet the minister, allegedly because he was not feeling good.'

Hrant was quiet while his mother was talking, as for Igor, with a hearty chuckle was nodding to his wife's comments.

Hrant said, 'you know, mother, you are omitting an even more important characteristics about Sara. The points you have enumerated are inevitably correct, but there is even more to say. I would like to attract to your kind attention to the fact that she is also a very committed girl concerning the Armenian Diaspora. She helps many of our movements, giving her time, her creative insight, and especially making use of her sociological advanced research, for a deeper understanding regarding the French, Swiss, and Armenian societies. Mihran's benefaction towards all different foundations and activities is evident, as you could observe during the years. So shall we say, like father like daughter! I am more than happy that I had to meet this wonderful family through your kind introduction. I am bound in gratitude to you both, and I hope you share my enthusiasm on this issue.'

'Of course,' was Igor's prompt reply. 'We are more than happy and thrilled that you got along with Sara, the daughter of one of my oldest and dearest friends. They stand for class by all means, and your mother and I are very proud to be their friends. They are so well integrated and respected citizens. Not only they are exemplary people in the Armenian community, but also in French society; where they are considered a hundred percent integrated and well respected citizens. They are highly educated, and part of the elite of the society, without being ostentatious, feeling very close to people of all standing, but their heart beats for Armenians. They think French, eat French, love and cherish their homeland, and feel proud to be part of the French nation and contribute to the welfare of the country. I can add, the same being true with the other Armenians dispersed in the four corners of the world, well integrated, reckoning their origin, trying to bring forth the bestowal of their ethnical and national realities. Trying to embrace in their everyday life the Armenian spirit, which is not a very easy task to do, to balance between integration and legacy; the same way we are dealing with our own environment, here and there. It is unfortunate to say that some Armenians around the world avoid these problems by denying their ancestral reality!' Igor glanced at his wife. 'Isn't that so, my dear?'

Maria, refracting the most romantic smile through her eyes, said, 'How sad it would have been if your family had not come to Switzerland? We could have never stumbled upon each other; you would have married someone else.'

'Well I call this destiny. I have met many beautiful women,' Igor said, now with a smile on the corner of his mouth, 'but I was attracted to you, my darling Maria. And besides, I would have found you somewhere around the world, I am convinced of that. Nothing is random. Destiny corners you by all means. Something magic crops up when two people meet; a kind of electric power is ignited. We call this attraction and others would call this the magnetism of divine intervention. In any case, why would you regret to marry an Armenian man, so humble and modest?'

'A prince by all means,' declared Maria. 'Yes a prince in exile, with no political power, only the incessant worry and sacred duty to look after his people's welfare as much as possible.'

Switzerland my love

Hrant was silent. Watching his parents' discussion, he was reminded of the generation gap, but he did not have a problem with that. He loved them and respected them more than anything in the world. He was enjoying the moment, having fun with his parents' discussion of love, power, and root. All these words he grew up with, were making more and more sense to his young heart. He was experiencing the most beautiful and rare feelings of his existence. He came to realise that he was blessed by the love of his parents. He felt a strong peace and joy in his deeper self; and thought he was so privileged and fortunate! Acknowledging the complexity of his situation as a prince in exile, with his alien origin, in a land where he was born and raised.

He felt he belonged to the country and did not need to integrate, unless his father and many of his generation that had to be accepted in the society and the country they were living in. No need to say that Hrant was committing his deepest allegiance, and respect for his birthplace. Recruited in the military service, he was ready to fight and die, to preserve the honour and the values of Switzerland. He had to practice the military service every year for three weeks, until he turned fifty years of age. That was the rule imposed for all Swiss males, in order to protect the homeland against all kind of danger. He had to live between pragmatism and root, richness by itself, a burden of twenty-four carat gold, pure and expansive, heavy and precious. To belong to many nations and to speak so many languages bears a different connotation; it is *le revère de la medaille*, even though he was prepared to play this role since childhood. The rules were tough, feelings were reasonably undermined, duty was alleged and endorsed, and it needed some concessions. He knew from his childhood, just like his other Armenian friends that he was different from other Swiss children. He had to be more responsible, stricter with himself, studious and diligent, strive to be attentive towards others, helping the needy and weak. He was an Armenian, and a prince, in a country where aristocracy was despised, did not make part of their history. Therefore, while the title itself was ostentatious, he had to maintain a low profile. Initially this was his natural disposition and demeanour. Hrant suffered no complexes, but some frustration and dismay was to play on his mind from time to time. He did not forget the appointment he had with the eminent historian, whom he had promised to meet and relate the story of his ancestors, which made him proud and was his reason to be.

Engaging with history: root, power and strength

Days went by. Hrant decided to call the Swiss professor. Sara was working hard in her final year at the university, meanwhile visiting

Hrant from time to time. In love and attached to her man, advising and encouraging him in his endeavours, patiently getting more evolved in his attributes. She attentively listened to Hrant, about his encounters with the professor, and his assignation. She was especially impressed by his engagement with the professor and their shared project. Trying to take as read and deduce the reasons and the objectives drawn into such a fathom tryst, apparently they were appointments of capital importance for both protagonists.

Professor Grimm was very happy to see Hrant after their last meeting. He was under the spell of Sara's personality. Her beauty and intelligence made a big impact on the professor, an alluring effect that made Sara blush, and Hrant swell with pride. He was just fascinated by the couple. They formed a conspicuous match of two remarkable glorious souls. After resetting his emotions and calming down his overwhelming feelings, he went on recalling once again with big enthusiasm the way Hrant and he had met in the train. 'We were meant to meet,' he said confidently. 'If not then, it would have been elsewhere, as would say *Carl Young*, the famous Swiss psychoanalyst.'

'Indeed, yes,' replied Hrant a smile on his handsome face. 'Are you suggesting that nothing is random, that everything is predestined? I am amazed that you believe in destiny. I thought intellectuals are more objective in their concept, having a rational and pragmatic approach to the givens of life.'

'Well,' said Grimm, 'you're right in that, one has the power and the freedom to control one's everyday life, and everything related to one's ability to make decisions. But then I postulate that big events like marriage, death, and birth, to name a few, are the projection and the extrapolation of unseen influences and energies that push us to the fulfilment of the issue at hand and its development.' After pausing for breath, the professor went on, 'our meeting is one of this oracular, propitious and opportune happenstance. Again, you are free, of course, to have your own opinion on these matters. I have an ardent desire to go beyond written history and live actual events told by a real protagonist; and here I meet you, my dear Hrant, along with your fiancée, a flamboyant and vivid prospect that I had not experienced before. Out of nowhere, we had to meet in a train that had to take you to France; and most amazing of all, we were face to face in the same compartment!'

'Yes,' agreed Hrant, laughing out loud, 'yes, that is how it happened; absolutely right, just as you describe it, my dear Swiss professor!'

Armenians and love, lingering between conservatisms, tradition and emancipation

'Last, but not least, my dear professor, coming back to our discussions about the nature and integration of Armenians of Diaspora, one should not undermine the issue of mixed marriages, coupled with its positive or negative connotations.' Hrant said. 'Love affaire is a very hot issue, a debacle more then ever in the Armenian Diaspora. This issue worried all generations for the preservation of the Armenian nation. They were tormented and apprehensive for the safeguard of their progenitors in regard to their Armenian heritage.'

The professor was absorbed by Hrant's view on love. 'However, there is such a paradox in this issue. Indeed, love dissolves all, challenges and contests, in view of the fact that one language is applied, namely that of love; which engulfs in it all the other attributes of compassion, comprehension, difference, tolerance and respect.'

'But when the time of countdown draws closer, dear professor, even simple algebra cannot solve the equation, of multiplication by subtraction; it is a quandary of consciousness for the new generation, especially when dealing with a nation that was decreased in number through so many massacres, wars and mixed marriages.'

'Well, Hrant, I fully understood your worry, but you should be more positive on this issue. By engaging and falling in love with someone of another origin, I am sure you're not losing one of your compatriots, but earning one more Armenian, as is the case with your mother. Isn't she as Armenian as your father? She has love and respect towards your father, thus she is married also to his nation! And what about Sophia?' The professor turned his attention to Sara. 'As far as I remember, I was told her father was French, married to an Armenian, her mother Seta. So you see, my son, it depends on the milieu and the people involved. Excuses can be created to support the argument, but it is always up to the individual to decide on his attachments.'

Favouritism, predilection, and prejudice

Hrant said: 'I genuinely believe, not jumping to conclusions, there is some truth about the loyalty of Armenian couples, the respect and humility towards their spouse and family. For them, the most precious and symbolic issue is the family, and then comes the homeland. I consider their moral fibre and their demeanour contributes to that end. Notwithstanding, this kind of character is usually forged pertaining to the environmental and social givens. Our social life did wrestle with its historic reality, but walked parallel with it at all times.'

The professor nodded, and Hrant went on, 'Another burning issue is the reality of our history, and the reasons why and when the Armenians of Anatolia, the little Armenia, the citizens of the **Cilician Kingdom**, gradually were carried out, unleashed, embattled, and during centuries were inflicted the rule of contention and contempt. Having lost their kingdom, they fought for centuries with courage and determination different feudal lords, caliphs, and emirs. They were forced, through the rivalry and dispute of different powers, to become an ethnical group.'

By this time Hrant was tired; obviously the subject he was dealing with, was an emotional one. The theme at hand was consuming all his energy. He was dealing with the Armenian characteristics, referring to commendable and illustrative dates, personages and places, partiality, predilection and prejudice being the major denominators.

Aware of Hrant's tiredness, the professor wanted to bring to a close their meeting, but our young prince was intent on continuing.

'One has to take into account,' he said, 'centuries of accounts and memoirs of a competitive financial and cultural contribution of the Armenian people, who were most of the time under coercion. Everywhere they set out, they conveyed their small *hayrenic*, "Homeland." To them, that denoted their precious family! Their families and homes coincided with their homeland. A free homeland, sometimes becoming a far reaching dream, a longing, a memory, a subjective desire that had to move towards fulfilment, while the family stood as a light in the darkness, or a light among lights. The home, not only stood for shelter and protection, but also for the spirit of the milieu, becoming the sparkle, the happiness, the backbone, to deploy an identity. Getting deeper into the meaning, the word family in Armenian means *entdanik*, which is made up of two words: the root of the word stands for *"togetherness"* and the second stands for *"roof"*, so when combined they mean, *People under the same roof.*'

The professor was thrilled. For him all such knowledge and evidence was like the archaeologist digging and unearthing relics in the soil, coming up with small pieces of a statue that had to be set and positioned back together. Once assembled, repaired and restored, it would become a valuable museum piece, a valued piece of history. 'What a night!' exclaimed the professors. 'Thanks, my noble boy, thank you for these worthy accounts.'

Getting back to history with "the caliphs"

'Dear professor,' goes on Hrant, adopting a more revived and alert tone, 'during our discussions with Sara, especially alluding to our relation to Arabs, she was very much impressed by the Arab intellectuals and physicians of the middle ages, such as *Bin Khaldun*, who was said to be the "father of sociology and medicine". He had analysed human history through advanced social philosophy, by giving his theory on social conflict and solidarity and had contributed in depth to medical science. In regard to our history, considering and analysing our relationship with the Arabs, it is very interesting to see the influence that Middle Eastern Orientals have exerted on us, especially their influence on medical and philosophical fields.'

'My dear Hrant, I am impressed by how interesting this topic is. Do tell me more, I am so eager to recall all these events and names.'

'Well, professor, Arab Caliphate's great expansion on Persia and today's Arabic peninsula stretching from Iraq to Egypt, Syria and Palestine, started after they converted to Islam in the 7th century. It was the awakening, the most influential and flourishing period of the Arabs in general. They entered the Great Armenia around the 8th century AD, and occupied the territory for some 200 years, giving some autonomy to the local governing powers. Some of the caliphs allowed the very powerful noble families, like the *Arzrouni* princes, to rule the country, letting the Armenian people enjoy freedom of religion, and thereby conceding, and giving way to the fact that Armenians were very faithful to the Christian religion and the usage of their language.

'Is that so?' remarked the professor, thoughtfully.

'Yes, it is important to revise our past history, to understand better' President Jacque Chirac's references to the Armenians of Yerevan. I can sit here all night long to tell you about our history,' Hrant said with a big smile, 'but let me finish the chapter on the caliphs, which is a very important chapter concerning the restoration of our kingdom during the 9th century AD. And what followed had a direct impact on our history during the middle Ages. As I said, the caliphs in general treated the Armenians of Greater Armenia well. On the other hand, there were some caliphs, who tried to convert our princes and Nakharars (Dukes) to Islam. The saddest issue was that they forced our virgin girls to marry them by use of force or by kidnapping them.'

'That is indeed an awful historical fact,' agreed the professor.

'We always hear about kings and caliphs willing to abduct virgin girls!'

'I am sure you know the reason behind this, my dear Hrant. It has less to do with moral attitude than with medical well-being. I mean, to express myself more clearly, it has to do with health! According to medical history, Arab men in those days acknowledged a virgin as being pure, and therefore to be harbouring no communicable disease. I ask your forgiveness for being so rough and direct on drawing on this historical fact. But in ancient times sexually transmitted viral disease was a major cause of early death. The mortality rate was high. Unfortunately, even today, although diseases such as syphilis and gonorrhoea pose less of a threat, we now have the curse of HIV and AIDS. So not much achieved, the problem still exists. Hopefully people are better educated and more aware now, and thus able to protect themselves against such inconveniences. I hope there will no longer be any need to abduct virgins!' concluded the professor, which led to a hearty bout of shared laughter.

'To come back to the historical recount,' said Hrant 'the relation of caliphs towards "Motherland, Greater Armenia" and its people. Some caliphs did not stop there. Every now and then, they tried to suppress and intimidate their subjects. A good example is the caliph of Baghdad around the 9th century, *Abed al-Malik*, who sent his commander, *Yussouf*, to usurp and kill the rebellious Nakharars. Do not forget, my dear professor, that our people were not cowards; they did not want to feel subdued. They always wanted their own kings and nobility to rule them, so from time to time there were rebellious uprisings against the usurper. It was during one of those rebellions that the caliph wanted to wipe out the aristocratic ruling body. So one night in a surprise assault, he and his army bore down on four hundred noblemen. Then he forced them into one of *Nakhichevan's* churches, entrapped them, and then burned them alive. It was a grievous, mournful event. The Armenian people were left in a most disarmed and chaotic state, their leaders burned to death after heroically resisted the caliph's will, whose sole purpose was to convert them into Islam. The Arab historians registered this episode as "The year of great burning". *Pope John VI* had quoted the event, describing the aftermath and emotional reaction and vexation of the people of Armenia thus: "Ocean of tears flooded Armenia".'

'For some time the Armenian people were disarmed and distressed. They were left like sheep without a shepherd. But the rebellion of the Armenian people continued, every now and then the caliph sending new commanders to control the territory. One time, very furious, the caliph sent a huge army commanded by a chief named *Bugha*. He was a former notorious slave, detestable and loathsome. Owing to his despoiling and despotic attitude, the natives of all the provinces, especially in the Armenian cities and territories, fended him off. He was destroying and ravaging, decapitating, setting ablaze many citadels and fortresses, implementing coercion and bloodshed upon the territories, whichever he was crossing by. He was so cruel that history named him "The Butcher". Bugha seized many Nakharars as captives and sent them to Baghdad to the caliph.'

'Terrible,' whispered the professor.

'Notwithstanding all of this,' continued Hrant, his gaze full of emotion and his young voice adopting a more intense tone, 'our Armenian captives insistently refused to accept Islam as their religion. The caliph, angry and disappointed that neither force nor intimidation could make the nobles change their conviction, then ordered them thrown into dungeons and tortured till death. The leader of this heroic group was, Sempat Bagratuni Sparabet, an influential governor of Armenia, who together with many other Armenian nobles, was killed for having spurned the caliph's command, choosing freedom of faith and freedom from prejudice. But, thank God, not all Arab caliphs ruled in this way. One decade later, Armenian subjects were at last able to enjoy autonomy, and long lasting peace under Arab authority. It was under the rule of *Ashot Bagratuni*, the son of Sempat Bagratuni, that the Armenian population could again live peaceful and prosperous lives. He was proclaimed Prince of Princes, being a sagacious, keen-minded, sharp and perceptive politician, though not, unfortunately, well regarded by our kings and princes in general, as history can witness. Thus, the Armenian kingdom was eventually restored. Ashot I was crowned king of Armenia, with the backing and blessing of both the caliph and the Byzantine Emperor *Basil I*, who was of Armenian descent too.'

'Actually, many Armenian kings ruled the Byzantine Empire during the Middle Ages,' commented the professor, knowledgeably.

'On the day of the coronation' continues Hrant, 'the caliph sent King Ashot a crown and many precious jewels. Basil, the Byzantine emperor, sent a golden cross, ornate with pearls and precious stones. I was also taught that according to aristocratic tradition of that period and many centuries after, during a coronation ceremony of a Byzantine king, Armenian kings - especially representatives of the Bagratuni royal family - had the sacred duty to solemnly lay the crown on the new king's head, as an acknowledgement and gratification of strong ties.' Hrant paused and looked at his watch. With a pronounced sigh, he said, 'I'm afraid I have to leave you now, my friend. We will see each other tomorrow as we decided. We will have lunch together and then proceed with our discussion.

The Armenian woman

The professor was very curious about Armenian women. During one of their meetings he had alluded to Sara being a graceful and charming person.

Hrant smiled. 'Well, professor, I would like to thank you on behalf of my fiancé. Without being conceited, I can safely say they are known for being attractive feminine women, tidy and clean, conscientious human beings, just like Swiss women, devoted to their families. Armenian women are also very fashion conscious. They are invariably smart and careful in their choice of attire, always projecting their inner feelings towards beauty and comeliness. The Armenian women of the 21st century are doing their best to harmonise their beauty with the western standard, the general accepted beauty of our times. They walk hand-in-hand with our modern era, sculpturing their body and keeping or bringing about perfection. Their style and beauty has no boundaries. Every modern citizen of the world, especially those of the developed countries, hanker after the cult of health and beauty, and Armenian women are no exception, conscious of ageing with stateliness and dignity, thus controlling the ageing process by trying to age gracefully, in good health and harmony through nature.'

'Once a dermatologist underlined to me an important issue regarding the skin of different nationalities,' continued Hrant enthusiastically. 'He alluded that Caucasians, especially Armenians, have one of the best skin types. Their skin is soft and shiny, does not wrinkle easily. I had not met Sara then,' Hrant added with laughter. 'It is a national trait, a token which is so much appreciated and sought after, when we want to look young and comely, without any medical interference. Blessed through nature and specified through our genetic "good quality cellular cohesion". A fortunate issue, I assume. Armenian women are also known for their practical intelligence and youthful maturity.'

'My eyes tell me that is easy to believe,' was the professor's polite response.

'As well as their acquired intelligence through education, attending colleges and universities on an equal footing with women of the leading western nations, they now encourage their children towards that end. Throughout our history Armenian mothers had their special status within the family. Committed mothers considered being the queen, the fire, and salt of the household. When beauty lost its footing from their physical body, it was superseded and taken over by their wisdom and acquired experiences. There are more poems and songs written on mothers, in our small nation, than any other nation. Maybe next to us are the Italians, but I'm not so sure about that. They valued their partners and tend to be more loyal than most occidental women. I wonder if this is because of education or environmental influences, or sometime both? Questioning and observing many women around me, I found out that loyalty is even genetic. Well, I cut short on my inquisition on this issue and accept the result as a positive output, in a world where divorce and pluralism are one of the hottest issues of our times. Their sacrifice and gratification is reflected through their progenitors. They cherish their children and think they have the best children in the world.' Hrant smiled wistfully. 'We forgive their exaggeration on this issue. Having a subjective stance, an assessment factual to their motherhood, and thus to their enamoured, unconditional love!'

Digging up the root of history

'Actually,' piped up the professor during one of their regular meetings, 'I know many episodes of the Armenian history, archived during my doctorate period. I had to go through the very complicated Armenian history, related to the history of Asia Minor, which I must admit has a history more complicated than that of we Swiss.'

This said, they both laughed heartily, unsure if it were the fact or the bitter truth that made them laugh.

The Professor continued, 'I know that the origin of Armenian history dates back to around 2500 years BC. The Armenia started under the rule of the kingdom of Urartu, intermingled with many groups such as the Arameyans and the Parthagenians from surrounding regions. With *Tigran II* the Great, the Armenian kingdom was well established with its strong influence in the regions of Asia Minor, stretching to the territories of Macedonia until today's Northern Turkey, Nagorno-Karabagh and Syrian territories. Its empire was gradually weakened by the constant invasion of Romans, Byzantines, and Turkmen from the north, finally falling under their rule.'

'Yes,' Hrant said. 'We have Armenian settlers dating from that period. They call themselves old Armenians - a term which denotes that they were in the lands around Asia Minor much before the kingdom in Cilicia was established.'

Armenians betrothing Christianity

'Armenians were the first state under the rule of king *Deretad* in 301, accepting Christianity as their sole religion through Krikor the Illuminator,' Hrant told the professor. '*Krikor the Illuminator* (Loussavoritch) baptised the Armenian people, with their king and aristocratic circle, in the Euphrates River. Effectively, it would have been a breathtaking scene just watching hundreds of thousands of people marching to the river, to be blessed for the eternal life, by the sacred baptism in the name of Jesus. To walk towards a new door, a new illumination that had to draw the line between his neighbours, who had acquired another religion, but paradoxically were calling the name of the same God from their minaret, or from their synagogue! The outcome was very bad for the Armenian people. Their neighbours declared incessant battles and wars against Armenians; and for centuries to come, they were being punished for being different, by the use of daggers and destructive fire.'

The professor nodded his agreement. 'That is so.'

'Today at the threshold of the 21st century, Krikor the Illuminator acquired one more acknowledgement and a merit, this time from the Catholic Church. A sanctuary was set up in the Vatican Place. It was an homage rendered by *Benedict XVI*. His marble statue is sitting conspicuously among other saints of the Vatican. The churches left by Armenians in Persia and eastern Turkey, mostly in Constantinople, about four hundred of them, with the very typical Armenian architecture, including those in Anatolia,' goes on Hrant, regret in his voice, 'are the remnants and implemented endorsement of our short-lived kingdoms. The area of Mount Ararat, *Kars, Ardahan,* and mostly in the old city of *Ani* and many, many other cities like in *Jurfa* near *Esfahan* in today's Iran, in Crimea in Calcutta, and mainly in Georgia especially in the city of *Djavakh*, from East to West. These fortresses and churches are a monumental and tangible reminder of the past vestiges of Armenian history. Armenian architecture has influenced the occidental Gothic architecture for many centuries. Armenians, wherever they went, first built a church, then a school. Many museums in Armenia and most big capitals in Europe - especially the *Louvre* in Paris, Moscow's *Kremlin Museum, Pushkin Museum* and the *British Museum* in London to name a few - are filled with antiquities, books ornate with silver and gold, so divinely crafted, and refined saint books and Icons, denoting our past heritage. The *Khatchkar* sculptures in the form of a cross, found wherever reminiscence of Armenian history walked from east to west of Anatolian and contemporary Motherland. All these Khatchkars carried secret messages denoting the fervent Christian appendage and love of its people. Sculptures, coins, paintings, precious manuscripts and liturgical objects, to name a few, all of which is evidence of the eminent role that our kings, our clergies, head of churches, the rural, the urban and the aristocracy played during centuries. The prominent contribution of the Armenian people, who were renowned for their culture, medicine, and religion in the history of Asia Minor and Europe.'

'But always there were many problems,' interjected the professor.

Hrant nodded sadly. 'Becoming the first Christians in the 4th century made us a crucial enemy in the eyes of our neighbours. Rivalry and religious zeal was another issue that the Armenian kingdoms had to encounter. Armenians had to deal with the intemperance of the Latin Papal states; also the Greek Byzantine Empire of Orthodox Church, both of different dogma, but bearing the same faith. Notwithstanding this, they had to suffer, too, the surging powers of the early Islamic empires, such as The *Fatimid*, the *Ayoubid*, the *Mamlouks*, the *Seljukids*, the *Tartars* and finally the *Safavid* and *Ottomans* domination from 1502-1928.'

'Yes, my dear professor,' continued Hrant, livid in a cheerless tone, 'religious extremism and fervent fanatic attitudes were the main issues, facing the rulers of those times. Christians and Muslims alike, voracious, and ravenous for richness and power, had implemented incessant conflict and unrest in the area, in the name of God.'

The following days proved equally interesting. Hrant was very excited to narrate details of his heritage, and respectfully remember the names of personalities, who had fought and died for honour. He acknowledged with great sensibility the memory of those clergies, who had shaped and defended the Armenian Church, playing an eminent role enhancing the spiritual and the political unity of the nation and the survival of its people.

'An example of a very conspicuous clergy is monk *Sourp Mesrop Mashtots* who created the Armenian Alphabet on the request of King *Vramshapuh*, late 4th century. Effectively, Armenian is a very rich language in the tree of the languages. It is as an Independent Indo-European language of the Cyrillic system,' explained Hrant. 'As a reminder, dear professor, Armenia being a very old nation, it was spoken of 2400 years BC. It has engaged in its vocabulary many other languages such as *Parthan, Urartian, Hittite,* and *Phrygian.* The influence of Hellenistic languages, such as Greek, and Latin, with the Romans is very pronounced. And the French influence, because of the relationship of crusaders with Armenians during the Cilician kingdom, and later on through the centuries. One can trace Persian and Arabic influences too, with their domination in the area. Some scholars say that the Armenian language is one of the world's seven great Indo-European languages. Just following the path of the language, one can trace the history and the civilisation of its people. What is rewarding for Armenians is that they have retained their national heritage from ancient times to the present, and that is gratifying despite the entire moral, linguistic and religious persecutions.'

'I understand from my exhaustive studies that the Armenian Orthodox Church was the backbone of the Armenian nation,' remarked the professor. 'It had and is still playing a major role in preserving the Armenian spirit and nationalism. Throughout the centuries the Armenian Apostolic Church (The name attributed for the Armenian Orthodox church) had to protect its people, enhance belief, hope, and universal love, wherever they were. With their ecclesiastical and heavenly blessed faith and devotion, they had tried by all means, to heighten the morale of their followers through harsh, difficult episodes, also exerting their influence in political issues, which was a repetitious and recurrent debacle in Armenian history. The Apostolic Armenian Church tried always to back, to strengthen and sustain its people, thus becoming the right hand of God on earth, gratifying tremendous faith. The best example we have is His holiness Catholicos Megerditch Khrimyan born in Van in 1820-1907. He is one of the most venerated figures for the Armenians. He was given the name "Hayrig" which means, "Father" because of his tremendous devotion and sacrifice towards his people. That is a very Armenian trait, I believe?'

'Yes,' Hrant concurred. 'In retrospect, our Christian religion was a kind of a lumber, a cause of inconveniences, thus making us weaker and isolated from our immediate neighbours. Most of our neighbouring countries had been converted to Islam. We had embraced a religion that was not the religion of the rising powers. Unfortunately, we had to abide and bear the responsibility of that difference for centuries. Just like in Europe in the Middle Ages, where Protestants and Catholics had to declare wars to impose their differences, wasn't it, professor?'

'Undeniably. Similar blind hatred towards religion till today,' was the reply of Dr. Grimm.

Armenians in the Middle East

'I'd like to underline, though, my dear professor, the fact that some migrated to many parts of the Middle East, either as captives, war prisoners, or pressured through the vicissitude of their lives. There were already Armenian minorities living around the Middle East at the beginning of the first millennium AD, as I mentioned earlier, regarding our King Tigran the Great. They were the families of soldiers carried by him. He had walked from the Armenian Plateau, crossing the boundaries of the Near East, today's Turkey, and Middle East. Some of them, a minority group, had been established in Syria, Lebanon and around the Dead Sea area, in Palestine, along with Greeks, Jews, Arabs, and some minority ethnic Christians.

In centuries past, they built a very strong church community, living in and around the city of Jerusalem and Bethlehem. They were mostly living around the city and in convents such as the convent of *St. Jacob* in Jerusalem, where the head of "John the Baptist" is still kept. The convent could host for about four to five hundred families of pilgrims coming from all around. It is said that, around the fifth century, the Greek Emperor Constantine, along with his wife Helena, built the first Basilica over the *nativity grotto* of the "Holy Child". Until today, the clergy of the Armenian Apostolic Church were the strong protectors of the holy sight for centuries. They are proud to own these most sacred relic spots of Christianity. They firmly protect their possession of the holy sites in Bethlehem. Actually, Armenians today, at the threshold of the 21st century, own the main setting and location of the church entrances, which led to the grotto of the nativity. The main altar of the church, raised on several stages, is situated over the crypt. From there on you can go to the grotto of the nativity through one or two entrances on the big stone stages which also belongs to the Armenians.'

'My father,' resumes Hrant, overwhelmed, 'was thrilled and so proud seeing all these inestimable riches in the hands of the Armenian Patriarchal congregation. Many times he thanked and eulogised the Catholicos and the clergy, who for 1,500 years, had protected their position in the enclosure of the sanctuary, despite many difficult moments, having to deal with grasping kingdoms, realms, and empires of all three religions. They showed detailed pictures of the birthplace of the Holy Child, which was highlighted and accentuated by a row of silver icon-lamps and fourteen silver stars bearing an inscription in Latin *"Hie de Virgin Maria Jesus Christus natus est"*, which translates as "Here Virgin Mary gave birth to Jesus Christ". And there are many other inscriptions in Armenian and Arabic. Today, after many fights over the rights of possession, it is being administered by the three confessions: Armenian Apostolic, the Greek Orthodox, and the Roman Catholics.'

'Effectively, my dear Hrant, the holy land was always under feud. It was a territory under constant dispute. Crusaders and the Saracens fought for many centuries. Henceforth, it became the main target of crusaders storming Middle Eastern territories, to fight the Saracens, the main power in those days, and capture Jerusalem, the Kingdom of Heaven on Earth.'

'Inevitably, for hundreds of years it was a deep religious problem,' commented the professor. 'Unfortunately, it was and it remains the main reason of dispute between Greeks, Catholics, and Armenians over the rightful settings of the holy site.'

'Well, my dear professor, I'm most touched and impressed by your detailed knowledge of the Armenian clergy of the Holy Sights.'

'You're very kind,' said the professor.

Legends to heighten the spirit and aspiration of the people

'Well, let us change the subject to a more vivid topic,' suggested Hrant, a little embarrassed by the uneasy fate that had been suffered by his Armenian side.'

'Skilled and hard working people are often under fire!' uttered the professor softly, as though talking to himself. Then, in a more animated voice, he continued, 'Well, my son, this is history, and nothing surprises me. History is full of bloodshed, treachery, unjust treaties, excommunications, and wars. Go ahead, enlighten my curious soul of things that I have not heard; also to liven emotions and passion that I want to enjoy through your stories.'

Hrant greeted this request with a laugh. 'Well, my dear professor I do not know about the emotions, but I am sure that you will get closer to the Armenian spirit and its people's aspiration, and eventually come to know the reason for our incessant migrations, just like birds that change lands to adjust their seasonal need. Each time thinking this is the last time, but was it? Let me give you a hint of our legendary heroes, professor. Are you conversant with them?'

'Unfortunately not, since legends, my dear Hrant, are narratives that people tell as a true story, but most of the time, the stories, the facts and the events cannot be confirmed, since they do not claim an eyewitness. They are made-up stories based on folklore, and I seldom came upon them during my serious studies. That's why I am more than eager to hear your version of these legends, which give breath and colour to its people.'

'Effectively,' explained Hrant, 'the sole purpose of these legends was a bestowal to the pride and spirit of its people, a fire to ablaze nations to brightness or demonise them to darkness. They nearly always contain a moral or message, to convey via their narrative. They tend to uphold and strengthen spiritual or religious values, and effectively contribute the spirit of chivalry. I love them, like the legend of King Arthur, which was developed over centuries, with more detail being added by *Sir Thomas Mallory* in the 15ᵗʰ century. It is the legend of a modest and powerful king and his magic sword that could be used only by him, since he was the strongest knight in the kingdom. He was surrounded by his loyal knights of the round table, most of all encompassing a beautiful queen, who he cherished and was very much in love with.'

'Yes, I am slightly familiar with that particular legend, Hrant my boy.'

'It is a story of passion and power,' continued Hrant, as an easy smile creased his handsome features. 'It involved chivalry, love, romance, jealousy, and some kind of magic, with certain folk appeal, especially in the Middle Ages.'

'Talking of legends, my dear Hrant,' set forth our professor, 'we cannot skip the very famous legend of Robin Hood. A legend, which was born in the middle Ages during the rule of Richard the Lion Heart. Robin Hood was a righteous man who fought against social injustice. He was the guardian of the poor. He fought against mistreatment and manipulation in the English city of Nottingham. All nations have adopted him, because of the basic principles he fought for. His example drew other justice-seeking kinsfolk, who conveyed the story to other nations. There are dozen of books written about these legends; and Hollywood has produced numerous films to be enjoyed by all generations.'

'I have enjoyed many of those films you mention,' smiled Hrant.

'Another famous legend is that of Guillaume Tell,' declared the professor, this time looking at Sara, who was sitting there listening to stories with which she was familiar, and wondering when was she going to learn something interesting from their conversation. 'Actually he is our only legendary hero of liberty, the pride of the

Swiss. The story of William Tell has influenced our neighbouring countries too, like Germany and France,' accentuating on the word France, to heighten Sara's curiosity. 'Its birthplace is in the Canton of Uri, in central Switzerland, which has one of the most attractive meadows in the world looking like emerald-green carpets, laid down by God. It boasts an awesome landscape. In springtime it gets even more beautiful with its lakes and backdrop of mountains that you might think, you have found Heaven on Earth!

'William Tell was a revolutionary, not willing to abide to the demands of the bailiff *Kessler*, who requested, or rather ordered him to doff his hat in deference every time they met. Of course, William Tell did not abide to his will. Upon this, the bailiff forced William Tell, as a punishment, to shoot an apple off his son's head with his crossbow. A cruel punishment in case he shall miss his target! Notwithstanding the risk, William Tell succeeded in hitting the apple, thus sparing the life of his son.'

'How cruel that bailiff was!' sighed Sara?

'Yes, and the aftermath was not tolerable for William Tell. His honour and pride were at stake. He became angry and revengeful. He decided to kill the bailiff, whenever he had the chance. One day, that chance arose, and he killed the bailiff, shooting him with his crossbow. In so doing, he liberated his fellow compatriots from the bailiff's harsh rule and regained their national respect and honour.'

'There is a chapel that was built around the 14th century for William or Guillaume Tell, near *Sissikon*, a small city on the shore of Lake Lucerne,' tendered Hrant, modestly. 'I visited it with my school and later on with my parents. We learned at school about him, when we were teenagers. In those years, we talked much about his heroic acts; for us he was a true hero and we were all his admirers. He had given hope to his kinsfolk against the *Hapsburg* invaders. Initially the legend became famous because of the German poet, *Friedrich von Schiller*, who rewrote the drama of Wilhelm Tell.'

'You know what made him even more famous?' asked the professor.

'Yes of course' countered Hrant. 'According to tradition, William Tell's heroic action against the counts of Hapsburg and all intruders, on the *Rütli*, created, the Oath of the "Swiss Confederates of Unterwalden".

Well, well,' smiled Dr. Grimm, 'So you know something about legends too, my noble boy.'

Indeed, professor. 'I owe to my grandma, my knowledge of the legends and many historical facts. Henceforth, I can tell you some of our famous legends, our folk heritage, legends that reflect the very character of our legacy.'

This time Sara smiled broadly. She was more than certain that she would enjoy Hrant's legends.

'Actually,' he said, glancing at his delightful Sara, 'we have two very famous ones that my grandmother used to narrate. The first is about our ancestor *Haig* and the Assyrian King *Bel*. Haig is our ancestral father, founder of the Armenian nation. Aram was his pedigree. Bel was a legendary tyrant of the area, who wanted to subdue and vanquish Haig. Bel had tried to impose some conditions on Haig by asking him to recognise his sovereignty, and by demanding his obedience. According to the legend, Haig refused to abide, for he was freedom-loving spirit. Therefore, after God destroyed the tour of Babel, Haig, our national hero, and his followers, all freedom loving spirits, faced Bel in a battle and killed him. But Haig did not stop his advance,' added Hrant, now aware of the professor's profound interest and curiosity. He migrated further to the north and established Hayastan (Armenia) - a free and secure land for his people to enjoy. This simple legend shows that Armenians do not tolerate slavery, or submissiveness. They have always fought for their freedom, for their land, inexhaustibly – the most significant issue for them always being the right to a free, peaceful, and prosperous land. The constellation "Orion" is named after our national father and patriarch Haig.'

'You mentioned two legends,' reminded the professor.

'Yes, this second legend does not talk of freedom, but speaks about loyalty to one's loved one.' Hrant again glanced at Sara, his eyes full of passion. 'It is the legend of "Ara the Handsome". In Armenian we say *Ara Keghetzig*; he was the son of Aram, the seventh generation after Haig. He was the King of *Nayree* (an archaic name for Armenia - today used as a pronoun for the feminine gender). Ara was praised for his capacity as a noble, a dedicated king. He was a particularly handsome man, with physically striking features. Everybody was attracted to him.' Hrant paused, again looking to Sara, this time straight into her eyes, with the most loving look that a man can give to his loved one. 'Armenians were proud of their handsome and devoted king. The fame of his handsomeness crossed boundaries, to reach to the Queen of Assyria, called *Samiramis*, who was attracted and infatuated by his looks. She desired Ara, crazed about him. She promised him half of her kingdom. Ara the Handsome declined her advances and refused her enchanting offers. Initially, he was already married; therefore, he did not want to betray his vow to his wife.'

Sara smiled at this, and Hrant said, 'Samiramis was a beautiful queen too, a charming, alluring woman that would make any man desire her and make him bend to her comeliness. However, our king refused to marry her, although he was under severe pressure to do so. The queen was upset and angry not to attain her womanly lust and desire. She was craving for Ara; but nothing could make him change his mind. So she declared war on *Nayree*. She wanted to pin him down, to succumb to her charms. She was a condescending, pompous, and arrogant woman, and knew how to make use of her authoritative position. However, to her deep regret, Ara was killed in the battle, even though her plan was to capture him alive. For long days and weeks she cried over his body, and prayed to her gods to bring him to life. But Ara had preferred eternal life. As a spirit, he had transcended his unfathomable loyalty to his family. And so his heroic action has been transmitted by word of mouth for centuries.

Part V

empires rollup and
generations walk off

Progeny of Roupinian, Hetoumian Bagratuni, Orbeli & Zakarian Princes and grand Dukes of Armenia

At their next meeting, Hrant had to tell the professor about the life of his ancestors. On the subject of the princes, and nobles of his direct lineage, the recounting of his great grandfathers and uncles, their itinerary and the lands towards which they migrated.

'*Igor*, my father's great-grandfather was born in *Crimea*'. 'His mother, Countess Isabella, was of direct lineage of the Zakarian's princes of Armenia from Sebastopol, which was the land of Tsarist Russia, during the reign of Empress *Catherine the Great*, around the 18th century.'

'After the fall of the kingdom of Cilicia (1078-1375), many Armenians migrated to different lands. They were people of all status, aristocrat or non-aristocrat, looking for a new settlement, a new future. Some crossed the sea, while others went to the inner lands like Georgia, Poland, Bulgaria, Russia, and Ukraine, also to Western Europe, mainly Italy, France, Netherlands and Germany. A number of aristocrats were already entrenched in those countries, deep-rooted through royal intermarriages and allies. The lineage of Bagratuni princes belonged to the same tree as their cousins - the Artzruni, the Kogovit, Oberli and the Zakarians princes of Armenia,' explained Hrant. 'After they lost their kingdoms and lordships, they were scattered to different lands, to find refuge next to a cousin of the same lineage, or to an in-law. Some of them tried to get involved in political issues, engaged in the desire of purng their political insight, by trying to get back their lost kingdoms and ranks. Others ran businesses, to flourish their cultural heritage. Generation after generation prospered in different lands, under different rules and decree and command, always facing the problem of powerful enemies, which led to terrible wars, during centuries! Sometimes, due to their rank and status, they had to endure all kinds of violence and unjust treatments. Being heads of states, they were under oppression, forbearing long years of imprisonment, made blind, or beheaded. Obviously, most of the time, they had been expelled from their kingdoms by harsh decrees, leaving behind their riches, their colossal possessions, and their lands - and sometimes even their families. Initially their influence and predominant role on the destiny of the Armenian Diaspora is of major importance, evidently their legacy of faith, survival and courage.

The professor nodded, but said nothing, anxious not to interrupt the flow of Hrant's narrative.

The young prince cleared his throat with a cough and went on, 'The Roupinian and Hetoumian dynasties of *The Cilician Kingdom* passed on to the *Lusignan dynasty*, who were the last kings and princes of the kingdom, till its destruction, end of 14th century. The *Lusignan kings* were of French royal houses. Mostly intermarried with -Armenian nobles house of Cilicia - another evident reason, why they spoke Armenian, French, and Latin. Their families had to run from the *Mamluk* insurgence and take refuge in Cyprus and unite with the kingdom there. Some of their siblings and cousins, through marriage, had been to Naples, Venice, and Aragon in France. The last king *Leo V Lusignan*, had the full protection of the French court and died in France, and was buried in *Père La Chaise*, the very prestigious cemetery in Paris.'

The Grand Duke Anastase

'On the other hand, the great uncle of Igor, the grand Duke Anastase, had made his choice by moving from *Crimea* (south eastern Ukraine), first to *Tiblisi* and then to *Baku*, where his ancestors the

Orbeli kings and nobles had reigned for centuries. All these cities, overtime, had become rich industrial entities, attracting huge number of emigrants.'

Anastase, on one of his visits to St Petersburg, decided to establish a home there, to be among his folks and in his aristocratic circle. It had an ambience and environment that he cherished, especially owing to the fact that the *Armenian Oblast* (province) has been created. It had a capitalist Bourgeois social structure, which lasted until the end of the 19th century. This newborn capitalist movement improved its relations within the *eastern Armenian hemisphere*, while in the *western Armenian territories*, like *Moush, Zeytoun, Van* and *Sassoun*, remained under the rule of the Ottoman Turks. They were oppressed and underdeveloped, desperately waiting for a big change and freedom from their Ottoman rulers. A foremost assumption and a capital reason had pushed Anastas to move to the East, establishing a new life. The Armenian nation was encountering effectively engaging in big political movements, while ideological assessments were roaring in from the west. The Duke wanted to work hand in hand with the tsarist government in order to help his people, making use of his political influence and aristocratic background. He was an Armenian Prince, familiar with the terms and tactics of the wars, notwithstanding the hidden demeanour of politicians, who had conducted the destiny of a whole nation drawn to ethnicity. He was aware of their pretence and deceit, using this or that argument, enslaving his nation for centuries. He hoped to adjust a rightful political stance to the Motherland to Gars-Ardahan, the Anatolian regions. Those regions, which were Armenian lands for centuries are now, through unjust and cruel political modification, losing ground. As the bitter result of lost wars, like "the Crimean Turkic-Russian war," lands were used for exchange purposes, obviously currency between conquerors, thus becoming guarantee pieces and collaterals.

'Russia and Ottoman Turks were the major perpetrators, the main leading   powers at the beginning of the 20th century. They were the leading antagonists, backed by leading European nations.

Weary endorsements were making the people on the lands confused and uneasy. Changing hands, like the cutleries of a dressed table. From dawn to sunrise not knowing whose dagger was to cut the throat of their neighbour, or which ruler was going to rape their daughter and steal their cattle. People of Anatolia were worried and confused by a baffling situation, unable to progress. Survival was the main aim of those people, who were desperately seeking tranquillity and peace. The urbanites, as well as the peasants, the clergy, and the scholars, all were hankering after a normal life, longing for a harmonious and stable era. They wanted to raise their children without having to encounter the savagery of a conqueror, or the unreasonable demands of a tyrannical ruler. They were tired of encountering misfortune, tired of seeing their lands looted to satiate the revenge of a ranking soldier. They were tired of being subdued to slake and quench the desire of an irresponsible warrior, who would burn entire fields, even towns, and thus annihilate the hard work, the drudgery of hundreds of peasants, who had toiled to nourish entire villages.'

Armenians dispersed in neighbouring lands

In the second half of the 17th century, the Armenian princes of *Artsakhor* - the so-called Meliks (Kings) of Karabagh - adopted the *Gandzasar Treaty*, which proclaimed the entry of Armenia under the patronage of Tsarist Russia. Attempts were made by the Meliks to bring forth some treaties, to protect the motherland, which was always under pressure from the bordering countries. For the occasion, the Meliks gave the tsar, *Alexis Mikhailovitch*, a commemorative token, a sumptuous golden throne encrusted with precious and semi-precious stones. To this day visitors can see this throne displayed in the Kremlin museum; a beautiful masterpiece made in Julfa (Persia) by Armenian craftsman.

Prince Anastase, in his helpful attempt, did not see the bigger danger that was creeping slowly but duly on the whole area. The birth of Marxism! It was the beginning of a new ideology, born in the mind of a Jewish intellectual. The socialist system, nourishing the communist era, was being drawn in red on the newly awoken sunrise, to draw the whole of the eastern hemisphere in "darkness at noon".

Although the theory was excellent, it proved unworkable dogma that bore no freedom whatsoever to the individual. Those who implemented the new regime twisted the ideology to the extreme, abusing the system and governing the people with an iron hand, resorting to coercion and cruelty on the gullible population to further their selfish aims. So Armenia had to encounter not only social and religious changes, but also physiological and geological transformation. In consequence, from one day to the other, they had to stumble upon the sad reality of newly drawn boundaries, which reduced their native country to half its historical size, leaving them poorer than ever. The cruellest and most unacceptable issue was that they were to be denied political and religious freedom. They were expected to toil for one purpose, to ensure the success of the new Bolshevik power!

Anastas' children, born at the wake of the 20th century, had to endure contemptuous attitudes and the implementation of callous social changes, and severe rules. They had to encounter the abolishment of the aristocratic appurtenance, a total social discrimination towards the intellectuals, who were all considered the enemy of the socialist central government. Those were dark days, especially for the Armenian nation, who was taken again between two swords - to be killed by the Ottoman Turks, or to live the harsh regime exhorted by the newly born Soviet empire. They had to bear this suffering by accepting the sickle and the hammer, or face death from a dagger, while crossing boundaries. Again, they were being forced to a contemptuous exile to foreign lands, to find refuge, hoping and yearning for better days. They were struggling repeatedly to live the nostalgia of their lost freedom and dream of their lost homeland. They were once again pushed for survival and adoption.

Migration towards Poland

Obviously, Igor's great-grandfather, *Leo*, was much luckier by choosing Poland as a land of asylum. There had been already a mass exodus to neighbouring countries. A flight from the severe occurrences, a continuous stream of the Armenian people, who were obliged to abandon their homeland with the hope and dream to go back someday.

From around the 13th and 14th centuries Armenians continued migrating from Armenia, running from the Mongol invasions to settle in the Crimean peninsula and in Moldavia. They had settled mostly in the South of Crimea, commonly known as *Armenia Maritime* Latin for Marine Armenia. Yet another wave of migration took place during the 15th centuries towards Constantinople, East and West Europe, especially in *Republic of Venice*, when the Tartars started invading the Crimean peninsula.

Large number of Armenians, about 50,000, who run away from Crimea, tried to settle in Poland, especially in the province of *Lemberg*, in *Lwow*, and *Leopold*.

In the 14th century, King *Casimir III* received the Armenians with open arms, and bestowed upon them honourable aristocratic titles, as well as allowing them to have their own national council. The Armenian Church enjoyed a welcomed independence and finally, in the 17th century, accepted the supremacy of Rome.

Armenian noblemen and commoners equally played an important role within the Polish civilisation. The Poles accepted their new Christian friends and gave them lands to start their new lives, especially around the city of Lwow, a region that became a real home for the Armenians. They were doing trade and bringing about intellectual and military reforms. Their Polish benefactors held these Armenian immigrants in high regard.

Among many cultural endeavours, is the use of the "Code of Laws". King *Sigmund the Old* decreed and implemented the Code of Laws, which was written in the 13th century by an Armenian scholar and priest, *Mkhitar Gosh*. The "Code of Laws" was mostly used under his reign, and continued till the region fell under Austrian rule in 1772

Leo spoke the language fluently. His family and his followers established their home in *Krakow* and embraced the culture. They got along with the natives, who welcomed and received them as valuable elements and representatives of the Armenian kingdom in exile. Effectively establishing a reputable colony in Krakow in hundred of years.

Today there is a small Armenian community, of peaceful and intellectual persons, musicians and *homme de letter*, who after hundreds of years of coexistence, assimilated with Polish through marriages. They are living in Poland in some of the main cities, especially in the Krakow area. There was also a very big Jewish community, very cultured and rich, who had migrated from Russia and Ukraine mostly. Leo and many Armenian businessmen traded satisfactorily with them.

The great-grandchild of Leo, *Duke Hrant*, had two sons, *Albert* and *Kevork*, and a daughter, *Mari*. After they graduated from their respective schools in *Gdansk*, all three of them attended universities in Berlin. His son Duke Kevork attended the Berlin Medical Faculty. His sister, Mari, studied biology. Albert, full of youthful dreams and achievement, had to cut short his architectural studies, to rush home due to a very severe infection. Unfortunately, his condition worsened; inevitably he was unable to return to Berlin to continue his studies. He had to stay home waiting to regain back his health. Until one day, his young and infectious body could not fight the free radicals anymore. Neither intelligence nor youth could maintain his health. He passed away at the age of twenty-four, at the blossom of his youth. Henceforth, becoming a star among the celestial stars, to illuminate his people from above, in the darkness, twilight, and dusk. The loss of their loving son was a terrible blow for Duke Hrant and his wife, but Albert's short life is remembered to this day.

Kevork, on the other hand, became a renowned surgeon. He had a very curious and adventurous character too. Being a bachelor, he liked to roam and visit many different countries. Once, during a trip to Switzerland, he visited Geneva and Montreux, and he was much impressed by their natural beauty: the high-pitched soaring mountains, the emerald green meadows, and mostly the lakes. He was particularly drawn to the French-speaking part of Switzerland. Finally, one day he decided to migrate definitively to the land of his desire. He had written to his parents about his urge to establish a permanent home in Geneva, inviting them to come and live with him in his beautiful villa on the shore of Lake Leman. A paradise on earth, he had written to his parents!

Duke Kevork had no problem of integration. He already spoke French fluently, since he had French blood from his father's side. So from an early stage, all the Bagratunies and Arzrounies spoke Armenian and French, by and by the language of the host country. The duke married an Armenian aristocrat from the Orbeli dynasty. Their children, Igor and Sybilla, grew in the spirit of their family, nurtured and encouraged with a Helvetic education, while reserving their right to render homage to their heritage and recognition to their ancestors. After finishing collage, Igor attended the university of Geneva, became an architect, like his grandfather Hrant, to overcome and compensate the motivation, and fervour of his passed away uncle, Albert!

Igor and Maria

Having recounted all of these facts to the eminent professor, Hrant continued with enthusiasm to enlighten him further, accepting the fact that the names of the pedigrees were sometimes confusing.

'My father, Igor, met the queen of his heart Maria, a student from the School of Art, when they literally bumped into each other in the doorway of the library. 'Consequently my father used to recall,' goes on Hrant with enthusiasm in his voice, 'bunch of papers slid from the young woman's hand and fall to the floor. Igor, (my father) after apologising profusely, laid his eyes on Maria's young, bashful face, blushing even more under intense gaze of a dark haired, young student. He instantly noticed her flawless fair skin, where were drawn the most beautiful blue azure eyes, on the verge of tears. Ill at ease, she was all the way repeatedly apologising to him, blaming her clumsy attitude. Igor on his side was amused and enchanted. He stooped to collect up the fallen papers along with the unnamed student, whose cheeks were changing from rosy to red blossom, feeling the closeness of my young, charming and banter father. Well nothing is random, as you said last time my dear friend,' says Hrant, again cheerful, 'obviously the story of my parents is the strong evidence. Some unseen elements push us towards a certain fulfilment. When it corners us, it is up to the individual to grasp the moment.'

Dr Grimm merely smiled.

'From that moment my father could not detach his eyes from her face, neither in his daydreams nor in her presence. He decided to marry her before someone else would take her from him. Apparently, this was a genetic concern, a worry that upset them deep inside, to hasten and to put love before duty. His ancestor, "Prince Toros," had pledged the same attitude, summoned to marry hastily his first sight love, putting his passion before the crown when he met his princess, "Alexia". Maria was a studious and cheerful young girl, very spontaneous and keen on her ideas. She was proud to belong to generations of an old Swiss family, of modest background, herself of reserved parents well versed in the arts.'

'Sounds like an ideal match.'

'You would think so,' said Hrant, 'but the duke was not very happy with his son's choice. He was eager and expecting to see him to marry an Armenian woman of aristocratic descent. He was hoping to marry Igor to the daughter of his best friend. The idea had nourished both men for years. However, Igor's choice was unwavering. He was deeply in love with Maria and wanted to marry her as soon as possible. He did not want to make any concessions, nor see or accept the reality of his heritage. He was the eldest son of the family, so had the burden to carry the lineage, which seemed to him like a cross on his shoulders, rather than a throne on his head. Nonetheless, there were moments that he was ready to renounce his title. It took him a while to convince his parents, promising them that they were gaining a daughter. 'She deserves your confidence and consideration,' he told them determinedly. 'She is ready to learn our ways, carry my heritage, appreciate and value my roots. We love each other and therefore we accept each other's differences and will make the best out of it.'

'A strong-willed man, your father,' remarked the professor, nodding his head.

'Yes, but it was a difficult time for him. One day the duke and the duchess sent a bouquet of roses to Maria, inviting her for a dinner. My father, fearing the disapproval of his parents, was worried about the outcome of the meeting. He had to introduce Maria to the most conservative old couple, who were deeply and wholeheartedly rooted in Armenian tradition and root. He was praying that they would give their support and approbation to the woman of his choice, even though it did not satisfy their traditional ancestral expectations.

She was so graceful, so lovely, this young Maria, my mother to be, father used to recall. 'She was standing there in her simple gown in dark blue, revealing the deep blue colour of her eyes. Her golden hair was shining like silk under the sparkling light of the chandelier at my parent's living room. She stood there timidly, obviously full of dignity, answering politely their probing questions. Even though she made a good impression on both my parents, nonetheless they needed to make many concessions to accept and bless our union.

'However, goes on Hrant again, finally they give their consent, agreeing to the marriage, once my father had completed his architectural studies. Effectively, abiding to their parental authority, my father received his diploma!'

On one beautiful winter day, warm and bright, they said, "yes" in an Armenian Apostolic church. Relatives and friends had rushed from all over the world, assessing their commitment and love for the new generation. There were more than ten languages spoken by the guests attending that ceremony. My father, Prince Igor, is a living example of an exiled prince of Armenian kingdoms, of itinerant ancestors, of an aristocratic descent. He was not much known or anxious to be acknowledged. He never introduced himself as a prince. His credentials were his personal pride, denoting his ancestral heritage of which he is so proud.'

'A fabulous, outstanding story,' said the professor, smiling warmly.

'Regarding my own position, my dear professor, I am more on the scene. Momentous occasions are driving me forward. I grew up intending to retrieve my lineage publicly, to implore and revive the dignity of a nation, their achievements in the overall history of mankind, the contributions of our kings, generals, soldiers, the exalting and heroic role of our queens. Some of them were queen mothers, like Princess Doleta, Queen Isabella, Queen Kir Anna, Princess Alexia, Princess Sibyl of Antioch, to name a few, all serving with intense vibrant devotion to their people, so often wretched in desperate schemes. As meritorious leaders they fought for their people, at their husband's side. Living moments of dire plight, facing great hardships as they fought for their liberty, for their land, and for their people, especially for their religion, they loved their people, and fought for the children of Armenia.

Part VI

The Armenian question and swaying relations with the Turks

'Dear professor,' Hrant said, revived after a short break. 'It will be very unreasonable to explain to you the major traits and events of our past, without telling you about some of the atrocities of our recent history.

Dr. Grimm mouthed a sad smile. 'Yes I know, my dear Hrant, of course I am aware of what you want to point out. That part of your history being relatively recent, all newspapers have alluded to the issue, without making clear judgement on the matter. Yes, of course you want to talk of the genocide of 1915 by Osman Turks, which is still a disconcerting and unresolved issue for the Turkish nation.'

'Effectively my dear professor,' continued Hrant, 'I grew up with this unresolved issue always present. It is a subject of concern for all Armenians in the world. It is vital to them that the Turkish authorities formally acknowledge responsibility for the massacre of Armenian people by the Ottoman Turks. It is a controversial issue, which is creating a polemic. Do you realise, my dear professor, that the new Turkish generation does not even recognise those past events? Many of them have an attitude of contempt towards my nation. It is an infamous segment of their past history, which is being hidden from them. Because they are largely unaware of what happened, they are much surprised by the present-day attitude of the Armenian youth! Therefore, I consider this unresolved issue a matter for serious debate.'

The professor nodded grimly and said, 'Your role, my dear Hrant, is to try through your conspicuous, pacific stance, as an Armenian prince who bears the vivid consciousness of a nation, effectively being the influential voice coming from the very far end of Asia Minor, to contest instigate and implement your truth, with conviction and veracity.'

'Yes, professor, that is indeed my intention.'

Weighing his words carefully, the professor said, 'I, as a neutral Swiss citizen, very much think you should try using factual evidence, of which there is much to explain to the new generation of Turks and make them understand that yes, these massacres did occur in 1915 and are an ignominious blemish on their so immaculate history of Ottoman sovereign power. Sooner or later, they will have to acknowledge the reality of these shameful barbaric events at the beginning of the 20th century, and atone for them. As a Swiss historian with a detailed knowledge of the treaties and events of that turbulent era, I think they cannot escape to acknowledge these dark events of their past. They have to admit and accept a very big wrong, was committed by the Osman (Ottoman) supreme leaders. It was clearly genocide, a planned massacre and deportation that was not solicited, nor condoned by most of the Turkish people of that time. I fully understand the despondency of Armenians and their disappointment towards the denial and irresponsible attitude of today's Turks. Armenians, old and new generations alike, are waiting to this day for a sincere apology, before their attempt on the second step of reconciliation and friendship.'

'You speak wisely, professor, for that is indeed so.'

Undeniably, my dear Hrant, Turkey is a big Nation and as such has to admit and turn the page on its past the way did Ata Turk by modernising Turkey. He turned the page and redeemed on old Turkey, but he ignored that very important issue - the Armenian question, as well as the related questions of Greeks and other minorities.'

'My dear professor, the paradox, in this entire historical juncture, is that Armenians had a long-lasting friendship with the Turks for so many centuries, well integrated, being very close even though not the same. After the fall of the Cilician kingdom in the 14th century, thus losing our leadership, we fell gradually under the domination of the new rising powers. We were committed to become ethnical groups, dispersed here and there in Anatolia and other big cities, like Istanbul. Obviously my dear professor, the historical name of Istanbul was Constantinople, incorporated in the Ottoman Empire, by Mahmet II the Conqueror. It became the new capital for five centuries until the fall of the Ottoman Empire in 1923. It is a fact that Armenians did feel enslaved in a country that they felt was not ruled by their leaders. They longed to regain their original status, to revert to what was theirs, and tried to exert political influences, asking the help of big European powers of the times. Armenians had enjoyed a close relation with Europe through centuries. They had acquired high education and enhanced cultural contributions. Undeniably, they intermingled through marriages, thus bearing mixed pedigrees. Am I not a very good example?'

'Affirmative, my dear boy, just like you and me!' The professor was happy to see that Hrant had a big smile, ever since this subject was being debated. They both laughed, their humour tinged with emotion.

'Indeed my doting son,' added the professor, excitement in his voice, 'as I have told you when we first met, and I informed you about my educational background, I have dashed out my thesis on Asia Minor and the Middle East and I have devoted, drawn up large chapters on the authority of the ethnic people and their influence on the Westernisation of the Ottoman Empire. Armenians, along with the Greeks, Bulgarians and the Baltic nations together, had a political and economical influence on the sultans. At the beginning of the 18th century, eminent Armenians of bourgeois society - architects of the Balyan dynasty - designed and built palaces, public buildings, banks, schools, churches, barracks, and mosques. Most notable is the beautiful Dolmabahca Palace, built by Nigogos Balyan in 1848-1856. There were many other eminent figures of that period, the list being long.'

'Indeed it is,' Hrant said solemnly.

'Talking of banks, since you are a banker, my dear Hrant, there is a good example I can think, namely the Sakarians and Artin Amira, big bankers, who became so powerful that they lent money to the sultans. They earned the title of Amira (Prince), awarded by the sultans as a reward for their great contribution. All these evident and huge contributions during the 18th and 19th centuries gave a status of privilege to the upper class Armenian minority in the Osman Empire. Undeniably, they were the instigators of the Westernisation of the capital city, Constantinople, which was becoming once again a capital worthy of its historic fame. Many Armenians had a privileged position in the parliament as ministers too. The sultans had appointed them as ambassadors and consul generals, to different European cities. Neither must one undermine their intellectual contribution as journalists, writers and as eminent professors in their universities! These contributions to the Ottoman administration cannot be denied or forgotten. Paradoxically, these positions and anks became a point of contention and jealousy towards Armenian, by the other minority ethnic groups living in Turkey, notwithstanding the Turks themselves. During that period many Armenians were living well, enjoying a privileged high status close to the sultans.'

'Oh yes, no doubt about that, but only in the capital and surrounding areas. Armenians living in Anatolia were not enjoying those constitutional rights or civil liberty, obviously that was becoming a major worry for our ministers and Armenian chiefs, who were appealing to the sultan on their behalf. They pleaded to the sultan, especially Sultan Hammid, beseeching more clemency and more autonomy for the Armenians living in Anatolia, in towns like *Moush, Sassoun, Zeytoun, Ourfa, Aintab, Kilis,* and the Cilician town of *Hajin, Marash,* to name a few, the list being long. Already sporadic pogroms were taking places in most of these towns around the 19th century! Of course, fate had no clemency for my nation. Neither plea nor diplomacy changed the course of events!'

There was a short silence. They were both in a ponderous state of mind; the subject was a serious one, arduous in its substance and a gruelling issue for all sides. A subject of moot and controversy, it necessitated a sincere apology and dismay from Turks towards the victims and their progenitors, which were born out of their aches! It was Hrant who broke the silence. He looked suddenly older than his age. There were many words not yet spoken, and many conditions not validated. He felt an urgent need to share these feelings with his knowledgeable professor, who was aware of the facts more than most Armenians. 'It is heartbreaking,' he said.

'Hear my dear son, I understand your dismay, the consternation of your nation, which was virtually destroyed en masse, eradicated. Your people forced to walk on the burning sands, hungry and naked. This was the systematic destruction of a whole nation, whose ashes were scattered all around the world and in the seven seas. The West and the major powers of the world know and acknowledge this reality, but again they seek their own political endorsements and political interests. We both are aware that the West was not always keen to intervene, seeing only a small ethnic minority, influencing and playing an important role near the sultans, having earned their trust by their loyal servitude.'

'Of course, it affected the tie by creating jealousy and the spirit of competition, not only vie a vie the Armenians, but also among Europeans themselves.'

'The turbulent era was gaining cause. Some westerners felt threatened by the power of Armenians, who were exerting a big influence on the sultans, to gain cause for their own problems. The West wanted to have control of the area, intensifying their treaties with the Turkish and fighting the Russians Empire! The circumstances and the state of affairs did not play in your favour from the West, especially taking into account that the First World War had started. The dices were thrown! I pray that my acknowledgement of this issue as a westerner, will enhance a light of hope in your young and worried soul.'

Again, silence.

Then Hrant said, 'The West reneged on its promise to help Armenians.'

The professor was a little embarrassed as he regarded the handsome Armenian-Suisse man sitting opposite him, thinking what kind of hatred sought to kill such comely souls, when they were so peaceful, full of humanity and faith. Lowering his gaze, he said, 'I hope that today in our civilised world, where everything is deeply analysed and overhauled, our politicians will take the right stance, to bring to justice the progenitors of these perpetrators, to recognize their terrible bloody episode committed against a laborious God-loving, creative people, who prayed only for peace, love and freedom.'

Hrant glanced at his watch. It was late. He thanked the professor and took his leave, already looking forward to the next day's assignment.

The next few weeks were very busy days for Hrant. Many Armenians of the new generation were preparing formal documents, to debate with Turkey's younger generation of intellectuals as discussed with his friend Dr. Grimm, trying to persuade them to acknowledge and accept responsibility for the genocide of 1915, the killing of innocent Armenians including mothers and their children, of one and half million souls.

The young Turkish intellectuals seemed friendly and eager to cooperate with Hrant and his friends, determined to find the middle ground to debate and resolve the historical mischief of their archives. However, such matters could not be resolved in only a few meetings, especially taking into consideration the Armenian elderly, who were more reticent and reserved in their approach to the Armenian cause. They were more susceptible, unforthcoming, henceforth harder. Reluctant, not willing to believe sinking of heart, to kind words of regret, full of qualms and scruple of conscience. Words they would utter, cannot fulfil out agony, nor reconcile with our past sufferings. We need action, which speaks louder than words.

Addendum Note: While I was preparing to despatch my manuscript to the publisher, several noteworthy, historically significant events took place, such as the very recent agreement of 10th October 2009, signed in Zurich, between Armenia and Turkey in the presence of major European and American heads of states. This politically induced agreement called for new cooperation, especially by reopening of the borders between the two countries. Both sides, especially the Armenians, were not entirely content with all of the clauses of the agreement. It brought about a polemic, since it did not mention either the 1915 genocide issue or the repatriation of Nagorno-Karabagh. But although it did not satisfy most of the Armenians, nonetheless, as the Exterior Minister of Switzerland, Madame Michelins Calmy Ray pronounced, it was a good start, implemented to bring to an end a century long dispute between these two countries!

The next meeting

Royalty's shared blue blood

At his next meeting with professor, Hrant was keen to discuss the lineage of Armenian royalty with the British Crown, especially with Lady Diana Spencer. 'For ten years now,' he told the professor, 'the British, and people of all nationalities throughout the world, have never stopped commemorating her premature death. The circumstances of her accident were never satisfactorily explained. Nonetheless, objectivity could never dissolve or solve subjectivity; doubts will always remain in the hearts of many people, especially the family.'

'Our Queen of Hearts is no longer among us, but she is in our hearts and minds,' declared the professor. 'Her beauty, elegance and simplicity earned her the utmost admiration of us all. She was a truly caring spirit, noted for her charity works and philanthropic endeavours. Physical beauty denoted by inner beauty made her the most popular princess ever.'

'Indeed, professor, and we all deplore that tragic loss. For me she denoted something special. I had dearly hoped to meet her, but she was gone and my words of thankfulness towards her royal highness were not fulfilled. So many times I was tempted to write to her, then I thought maybe such a step would not be in the royal protocol.'

'Why was that,' enquired the professor?'

'According to royal protocol, another member of the aristocracy must introduce me. Princess Diana was very democratic, but her entourage comprised several very conceited and very sophisticated members, not to say snobs. They were unlikely to have minimise the fact that I am not a British aristocrat, or belong directly to a European aristocracy.' Hrant went on, his voice wracked with emotion, 'She was also my princess and I insist on it. Especially ever since I had the factual proof that she was bearing in her genetic tree the same genes as mine.'

'Well, I am not surprised, Hrant, knowing the breadth of the British throne and their vast influence on all continents. Tell me more, my prince, I am more than fortunate to learn more about our world and its unfolded secrets.'

'Well, my dear professor, as you rightly assumed, dealing with many faraway lands, they had progenitors of mixed blood. Her pedigree of pure blood of Spencer ancestry was not pure English, since it had many other genes such as Hungarian, Russian, French, Armenian, and even American. I have proof that at one point, dating back some thirteen generations, a woman named *Elisa Kevork* or *Kevorkian* was of Armenian descent. Elisa Kevork belonged to a very rich Armenian family in New Delhi, and married *Theodore Forbes*, a Scottish merchant (1788-1820) who used to work for the East India Company. From their union was born a daughter, *Katherine Scott Forbes* (1812-1893), who married *James Crombie* from Aberdeen. The bloodline continued until the twentieth century. The grandmother of Diana married *Lord Fermoy* and their daughter married in 1954 the eighth *Earl of Spencer* (1924-1992) who was the father of Lady Diana. *Diana Spencer* (born 1961) married *Charles, Prince of Wales*, in 1981.'

'Amazing!'

'The personal file of Theodore Forbes is still in their archives and purports to contain letters in Armenian from his wife's brother. Some years ago, other such letters were discovered in the ancestral home of lady Diana ("Funny letters", since the Armenian language had its own alphabet of 36 letters). After investigation, it was realised that they were Armenian. They were letters written by grandmother Elisa to her children and grandchildren.'

'Oh, how fascinating, my dear prince, to hear all these revelations of your lineage! Indeed, I understand your excitement. The British are important, having implemented and played, in the past and present, major world role, in Far East, India, Middle East, Near East and Europe, for centuries.'

Armenian merchant princes of India

'En passant, I'd like to give a short account of the Armenian merchant princes of India,' Hrant began at his next meeting with the professor. 'They were the pedigree, the lineage of many aristocrats in Asia Minor and in Europe. Armenian traders, who already had a trade relation with Persia and India, settled in India around the 12th century, mostly on the Madras coast. Indian record trace that An Armenian merchant diplomat, by the name of *Thomas Cana*, had reached the Malabar Coast in 780, seven hundred years before *Vasco Da Gamma* reached the Malabar Coast in 1498. He was known as Knayi Thomman or Kanaj Tomma, meaning Thomas the Merchant.

These merchant Princes journeyed from Persia, through Afghanistan and Tibet, and made India their home. They were the first merchants to carry back from India, spices, muslin, silk fabrics and precious stones to the Middle East and Europe.'

'How interesting,' remarked the professor.

Hrant smiled, encouraged of the professor's ignorance on the subject. He continued, proud and fulfilled 'their contribution deserves to be mentioned. They were diligent people, with great potential. Over time, they became powerful and rich, and fully involved in the welfare of the country, in financial, political, and cultural function and position, effectively by building many churches, schools, and palaces.'

'That kind of commitment is in the Armenian tradition,' volunteered the professor. 'Whenever Armenians establish themselves in another country, they invariably manage to accomplish two things: first, they built a church, and then a school, so I am not surprised on the subject at all!'

'Well yes, my dear professor, how true,' concurred Hrant, excited by the professor's knowledge on the subject.'

'Not only that,' added the professor. 'They always followed that with other far-sighted and inspired projects, much to the benefit and happiness of the countries they lived in. However, my dear boy, please excuse my ignorance on the Indian issue. Not being aware that they had played such an important position in the Indian society and aristocracy as such, I am eager to learn more about their input there. Please go on, my boy, tell me about your Armenian princes of India.'

'I am proud to say, professor, that some of these families reached the ranks of princes and queens, ministers and generals through their intelligence, colossal fortunes, and commendable achievements. A good example in the 16th century, is the, the wife of the Great Mogul Emperor, *Abdul Fazal's Ain-I-Akbari*, the beloved Begum *Mariam Zamani*, she was of Armenian descent. Historians are not sure if she was the first wife of the emperor, but one thing is unquestionable - Mogul's love for his queen. He built a magnificent palace in *Fatechpur Sikri*, in her honour. The wife of Akbar's adopted son, *Mirza Quarnain*, was also Armenian.'

'I knew none of all this,' the professor admitted candidly.

Encouraged to go on, Hrant said, 'we are proud also to have a saint, a mystic scholar and poet named *Sarmad*, who lived around end of the 17th century. The empress Begum Mariam Zamani invited Armenian settlers to Agra. They benefited much from the emperor's consideration. These Armenian settlers were exempt from taxes and had the special privilege to move around in the Mughal Empire, where entry to other foreigners was prohibited. Armenian merchant princes of India lived in Agra, Madras, Surat, Calcutta, Saidabad - a province of Bengal populated by a sizeable Armenian community - and also in Mumbai, Delhi, and many other cities.'

'So many?'

'Yes. Another Armenian personality in the government of Akbar was *Abdul Hai*, the chief justice minister. Also worthy of mention is *Lady Juliana*, sister of Mariam Zamani Begum. She devoted herself to the welfare of the Armenians. Lady Juliana was not only beautiful, but also a doctor of medicine. The fame of her beauty crossed boundaries, extending as far as France. She was married to Prince *Jean-Philippe de Bourbon* de Navarre, of the royal house of France, and they lived happily thereafter. Yet another Armenian sultana or queen in the 19th century was the *Nawab Sultan Begum Saheba*, the wife of Mogul *Oudah Ghaziuddin Hyder*. She was as Armenian as I am.'

'Isn't Agra the city where the *Taj Mahal* stands?' asked the professor, picturing in his mind the geographical area of the prince's narration.

'Yes, indeed, professor, *Mughal King Jahan* built it in around 1631 for his beautiful wife. In addition, that is where most of the Armenian merchant princes resided for two hundred years; obviously, they also married their daughters to British colonialists. You will no doubt recall the example that I recited you, about Elisa Kevork, who married a certain British Captain Forbes.'

'Oh yes, how amazing! A small nation, dispersed here and there, contributing with integrity, conviction and generosity, to the welfare of mankind.'

'Thank you, professor. Yes, the contribution of Armenian merchants in all of India with their philanthropic actions is eminent, but unfamiliar to others. I recently learned from an Armenian residing in Los Angeles, who was born in Madras, that there were two brothers, very distinguished Armenian merchants in Agra in the 16th century in the name of *Mirza* and *Iskenderus*. They were cultural and social contributors to India, especially in Calcutta, in the north, governed and submitted to British mandate. Unfortunately today the north, especially Calcutta, is very poor, so inevitably needed the help of devoted saints such as *Mother Theresa*, who founded the "Missionaries of Charity" in the Calcutta slums, to aid and assist the terribly underprivileged communities in the region.

The professor remained silent, waiting for Hrant to continue.

'Mirza, our honourable philanthropy, had to suffer physical punishment from the emperor, for not denying his Christian faith. However, that fact did not stop him in his philanthropic actions. He and his brother built schools and churches. They encouraged architects, painters, and sculptors to great effect. Mirza also had the initiative to build a house for the pilgrims, visiting holy shrines, meanwhile following their faith. He also helped by donating large sums, for the needy Indian people around him.'

'At length, professor, I would like to enumerate about leading Armenian barristers, solicitors, archaeologists, and advocates in India, especially in Calcutta and Madras. There is also a nice story about an Armenian merchant named *Johannes Rafael* in the city of *Surat* in the 18th century. Johannes had a diamond of 195 carats, which he sold to Prince *Orloff*. In fact, the diamond was later named "Orloff". The prince, in turn, presented it as a gift to Tsarina *Catherine the Great of Russia.*' Hrant smiled and said, 'As I was going to talk to you about Armenians in India, I brought with me a very small writing of an eminent Armenian figure, *Thomas Malcolm*, who was the curator of the Armenian Church from 1837-1918. As of today in Calcutta, we read the following inscription on his grave:

> *Remember friends as you pass by*
> *That all mankind are born to die*
> *Then let your love on Christ be cast*
> *That you may dwell with Him at last*

Of course, there were many Armenians in China, Burma, Southeast Asia, and Vietnam too. Incidentally, I can say that an Armenian around the beginning of the 20th century started the famous shoemaking firm, Bata, in Vietnam. Subsequently you can come to evidence, my dear professor, about Armenians, who have been on the four corners of the world. Effectively, this monologue of mine is to illustrate my pride in my roots, without being chauvinistic. That's why I have tried, throughout our series of cordial meetings, to inform you about my pedigree, and their relation with the western royalties and the crusaders, especially from the 11th to the 14th century, during the Kingdom of Cilicia. The list is long, however, I can convey some examples. Our great king, Hetum II, also known as Prince of Lampron, was Lady Diana's 25th great grandfather. Princess Doleta of Armenia was Winston Churchill's 23rd great-grandmother. Another great Armenian queen, Elisabeth of Cilicia - was the pedigree of King George.

'Well, well, my prince, all this information about ancestry has certainly enlightened me, even though the names are a little bit confusing. You have made me fully aware of your rightful place in the Armenian aristocracy, and the undoubted linkage between Armenians and European blue blood.'

'Even though small, compared to the European kingdom and its aristocracy,' volunteered Hrant, modestly. 'The sole and unique purpose of my story is to bring to light the Armenian presence in so many fields, and their achievements in history dating back 2500 years, and the eminent role Armenian kings, Barons, Nakharars, princesses and its people played during the period of our short kingdom. I am more than proud and honoured, to know that I carry the root and richness of our ancestors on the path of history. In a word, our roots have the same implication, cradled and raised like all offspring. However, the difference lies in the upbringing, the environment, and the condition by which the seed of those roots have swayed.'

'My dear Hrant, I am sure those roots will, in time, attract due recognition and endow you with the power and authority, to further enhance the quality of life for Armenians everywhere, especially in Armenia.'

'Thank you, professor. I dearly hope that will prove so.'

Part VII

The Third Millennium

Hrant getting married

Hrant was elated. He was in high spirits, jubilant and over the moon ever since Sara and he had arranged a date for their wedding. Two years had elapsed from the time when they first run into each other. Both parents were impatient, looking forward for their blessed union. Sara had been to Zurich very often, from time to time accompanied by her mother, and occasionally, whenever possible, by her father too. Mihran found a new contentment in his visits to Switzerland, an incomparable opportunity to visit his doting friends more often, a delight mutually shared by Igor and Maria, and their future son-in-law, Hrant.

'Men,' Maria would say in a teasing voice, 'one should always run after them. So, my dear Sara, you have to organise your wedding accordingly, and then let Hrant know what you have arranged, *devant le fait accompli*, and most importantly, send him the list; I mean the invoice,' she corrected herself with a hearty laugh, shared by Sophia.

Sophia was helping Sara with the wedding plans, which she was sure, would ensure the most enchanting moment of her life. Her visits to Zurich were most rewarding, since she loved both, her charming in-laws-to-be, and the city itself. She implied after each visit that Switzerland was a very beautiful country and that Zurich was the most beautiful city ever. 'Small, but so convenient,' she used to allude.

'It is beautiful,' agreed Maria.

'Indeed, isn't it? Zurich has everything a big city should have. It is full of beautiful boutiques and stores, very modern with competitive prices, and ornate with historical monuments. It is a culturally endowed city. It has an opera house, two exquisite concert halls, where the leading orchestras and instrumentalists give recitals, and owns modern theatres. Effectively, Zurich can be proud for having more than two hundred art galleries for its half-million inhabitants. It is a continual enticement to artists of all kinds, from all over the world. It has an excellent commuting system too, (goes on Sophia with the same enthusiasm) which enables me to take walks to the town all by myself, enjoying a total liberty. One could find all kind of gourmet restaurants for every budget; and fruits from all over the world. Two big rivers cross the heart of city, while a majestic, transparent lake runs almost the entire city, mirroring all the surrounding scenery it its bosom, an enthralling, awesome scene of peace and joy. Zurich can boast for its harmonious atmosphere with its many nationalities, residing here and there around the state of Zurich, obviously, agreeably controlled, efficiently trying to integrate and engage in the green plan of the country, respecting the environment by adopting the system in their everyday lives.'

'My dearest Sophia, you forgot to mention our fine-looking committed policemen, and our seven Federal heads of state, each sharing for one year the seat of the president. Our parliament has wise and far-sighted deputies and ministers. Switzerland is proud to be a direct democracy; it is for the people and by the people. Even though very conservative and attached to their root, they manipulate the modern times with an incredible ease. They have adjusted to the country's birth of a Federal State since 1292, with its 26 states, and in 1848 the foundation of the state of Swiss under one banner. Amazingly enough, each state is a free state, with its own laws and the freedom to act and decide accordingly. Only major state problems and international questions are debated in the parliament of the capital, Bern!'

'We must not forget the problem of immigration - the unstable political and economical situations in the world swaying and affecting the influx so much.'

'Isn't this amazing and rewarding for a small country like Switzerland, to find so much order, beauty and coherence?' remarked Maria, joyfully.

'And a very rich country, full of banks,' quipped Sophia, cheekily, and they all succumbed to another bout of laughter, creating an aura of merriment and high spirits. Maria and Sophia got along like true sisters, sharing and discussing every detail of their lives, their children, including their husbands!'

'Woman-power!' Mihran would often declare simply, and Igor would glance in askance at Maria, to await her reaction towards the statement!

'Actually,' said Maria cheerfully, changing the subject, 'it is in the Armenian tradition, aristocrat or non-aristocrat, that the groom has to treat and take upon himself the matrimonial expenses, is it not, Igor dearest?'

'Yes indeed, no doubt about it,' came Igor's quick reply, his mind still hooked on the subject of womanpower. 'Our Hrant already is acquainted with the subject. On our wedding, I paid for everything, as is customary with every dutiful and compliant Armenian. Rich or poor, it makes no difference - it is a deep-rooted tradition. Initially it is Hrant's obligation and his sacred responsibility. I assume it won't be a painful duty for him. On the contrary, a real pleasure, I hope, and an opportunity to show his caring concern and unwavering devotion to his bride to be, to his loving fairytale.'

'Why is Hrant late again?' he enquired sharply, seeing Sara's edginess. '

'Well he wanted to visit our professor, so he asked me to excuse him tonight,' Mihran explained. 'Sara knows about it, no doubt, I am more than certain.'

Friendship hankered through recognition and respect

For sometime Hrant had been postponing his appointments with his friend, the professor Grimm. He was busy, and little bit lost mulling things over. He had too many things to organise and think about before the wedding! Inexorably, every time they both met, there was the same mood, vibes of intense disposition, the concern, and steadfast curiosity towards Hrant's ancestral story and events, proceedings and development of that heritage. Hrant had revealed the derivations of his Armenian roots, the complex history of his ancestors, and the enrolment of his heritage, the ways and the means of their survival. They were becoming true pals. In spite of their age difference, they had bridged the decades and conversed as equals. When they sat together, the professor and the scholar, the gap of years, inappropriate and untimely, would promptly dissolve. They would reincarnate into two ageless souls with brilliant minds, trying to cooperate and understand the depth of their mutual heritage: Swiss and Armenian through the centuries of complex and intricate discordant existence, which needed a strong character and tenacious attitude. It required a conspicuous stance, embracing will and determination, trying to remain faithful and committed to their roots!

Dedicated and passionate, they sought to bring forth resemblance through evident disparity, deem to appreciate the difference. Endorsing past aspirations by way of remarkable tenacity and fortitude, entire generations, ensuing the progenies of today's modern era.

'Both my nation, all along their history, proved to be strong-willed, tough freedom loving people' goes on Hrant to the professor. 'Very conservative patriarchal heads of families, who, most of the time, attest to be devoted, assiduous and loyal to their partners. Sometimes enticed to drink from the forbidden cup, indulging themselves, attracted and allured to the spell of beauty and youth, to obliterate the monotony of times and reluctance of age.'

'Both my nations (continues Hrant succinct) are famous for their ancestral, age-old agricultural products – the ramification of these products worthy of memory: such Grapes, cheese with tens of variety, and dried lean meat marinated with different spices, and made edible, once dried in its spicy coating, under the heat of the majestic sun. A secret procedure enhanced by special spicy savour, acquired ancestral expertise, and appreciated throughout centuries. These rural products, still cultivated and produced ensuing modern times, became a huge industry, with their diversified forms and taste, inducing a lucrative business for both my nations. As for the cultivation of Grapes, it is the consecration and gratification of the Armenia natives. There is a very traditional feast related to the grapes. Each year, "The Day of Virgin Mary" around fifteenth of August, the first harvests of grapes are being blessed during a church ceremony. Obviously, till today, all Armenian churches in the world, follow the same ritual of Grape blessing. Ancient times people would start eating the grapes only after the formal procedure of the consecration. In Switzerland we also have harvest feast based on non-religious rite, to express delight to their wonderful vineyards and the successful outcome of the grapes, in the production of their tasty wines. Actually I have contributed to grapes gathering many times, whenever solicited by friends. It is a wonderful feeling this oneness with nature. Realising how cultures subsisted centuries long ploughing the fields, being tough with their vigorous hands, thus nourishing entire communities with the outcome of their harvest, resisting capricious and harsh weather. Effectively flexible to change, both people had the concept, the aptitude to adopt and adapt to modern times, by tailoring the rural situation to suit urban conditions, requirements and needs.

This time the professor leads the conversation 'Switzerland owns beautiful meadows, vineyards, wonderful rivers, brooks and lakes that made our countryside a most charming lands. On the other hand, both our countries confronted and fought fiercely different enemies, struggling for their territorial, religious freedom and a neutral political deployment. They had had to thrive all through their history for peace and neutrality, protecting their boundaries from the insurgents. I reckon Armenians dispersed on many lands, they speak few different dialects; as for the Swiss, having many cantons, they have to deal with four different languages and dialects, such as German, French, Italian, and Romansh. On the other hand, when encountering coercion, they knew how to shelter and defend their national identity, uniting under one banner, singing all together their national hymn, to express their patriotic vibes, love, and devotion to their land.'

'Also, like the Swiss,' pointed out again the professor, 'I reckon Armenians were good bankers and they had their golden age during the 18th and 19th centuries. However, Armenians had one very special skill,' he added with a smile. 'They were very good businessmen too. They have long played an important role, inducing and cultivating a flourishing trade between East and West, with special emphasis on spices and precious stones, silk carpets and pearls. This proved very promising for some Armenians, who enjoyed ostentatious, flamboyant positions, becoming very rich and famous, such as Mr. Calouste Gulbenkian in the 20th century, engineer by profession, who lived in London later on in Portugal. He made fortune from petroleum, thus nick named "Mr. five percent". Tycoon and philanthropy, he established The Gulbenkian Foundation that sponsors all nationalities. We have also present day eminent, successful Armenians in the State, in France, Italy and in Switzerland.'

This last statement caused Hrant to laugh heartily, nodding his head as he reflected on those times. 'Well, there may be some other similarities in the sciences and architecture, too. The Swiss were luckier to reside with strong, knowledgeable, ambitious, yet clever enemies, at the heart of Europe. Their neutral political stance helped them a lot on conducting and protecting their country. On the other hand, Armenians were encircled from east to west, extending north to south, with unreceptive, aggressive and confrontational nations. Through centuries, they were challenging the territorial and religious reality. They were antagonistic tribes, constantly changing attitudes and sides, and heads of power. In a way we were unlucky, geographically condemned to live with belligerent people, leading to widespread instability. They were drawing and reconstructing new boundaries, creating hostile circumstances. They were argumentative and rapacious powers, positioning their rule by intimidation, always to the detriment of the people, expressing their will mostly with daggers, rather than the pen, and staining the lands with blood instead of ink. Armenians, professor, were the only Christians along with Georgians, throughout centuries to make any headway and repel the powers then threatening the Christendom'.

'It is a fact, I deem my son,' stated the professor.'

Hrant said, 'I feel very sorry and regret this undeniably fact of historians having undermined or minimised the role, the position and magnitude of our history.'

'Regrettably, even I, my dear Hrant, had forgotten much of that. I say today, Hrant, that I am most thankful for you having reminded me of these episodes. I am most grateful for having met you. You were my last rays of a sunset, disseminating and sprinkling more light on my historically piled facts. I feel most rewarded and fulfilled today more than yesterday, bound and devoted to my long career and lifelong studies, without this chapter in my portfolio, I would not feel fulfilled. To my sincere regret, unwillingly, I had undermined the most important role the kingdoms of Armenia had played, to safeguard Christianity. Unfortunately, many of my colleagues, both here and in other highly developed countries, not to minimise the presence of the man in the street, have undermined the true and important role and the effective contribution of the Armenian kingdom, which had remained unnoticed for centuries, a "Forgotten Kingdom"!'

'Quite so, professor.'

'I can add to this effective reality, my young friend, that you were always the prey of big powers intent on furthering their political interests before defending human dignity. Armenia is situated on the Caucasus peninsula, neighbouring Georgia and Azerbaijan. At the present time it is not politically strong, and is also a financially weak country, depending on foreign powers for aid. Intellectually, however, it has the aptitude and the talent to challenge big nations. Do not worry, son, all empires and kingdoms have an end, until the instigation and launch, the rise to power of new ones. I am aware that the Kingdom of Cilicia ended in 1375, but you still have your country, Armenia, which gained its independence in 1991 from the Soviet Union, enhanced with the collapse of communism. Armenia was their sixteenth republic. Amidst all kinds of atrocities and submissive situations, you are the voice and the pride of your ancestors and the gratifying newer generation!'

Hrant went home light-hearted. He felt he had accomplished a major duty by recalling his history, to a precious and important intellectual, who listened, also hankered and fell in love with the details and its people. He cherished his friend, his Swiss professor, and he felt proud to be listened to by him, even if others had no ear, or no heart to listen to the story of a small nation.

The Triumph of love and legacy

Hrant was almost running, looking at his watch. He was late; suddenly he had the utmost urge to be with Sara. Oh God! He was thinking, how I miss her, my princess, my beautiful doting woman. She was to become his other half, his lifelong partner. Effectively, the professor was to become their godfather. He was so much in love with Sara. For him she enhanced the perfect lady, unrivalled and unique. Her conspicuous and strong stance reminded him of *Princess Alexia*, the wife of *Prince Toros* of the *Hetumid kingdom*. He started believing in reincarnation, feeling the spirit of these two women coincide to the illusion of time and space. Obviously, she was a charismatic lady, dispersing similar passion and momentous strength like princess Alexia, who had dedicated all her authority and intellect for the welfare of her people!

While driving home, he knew he had a tryst with destiny. Among his detailed matrimonial preparation, he was seeing himself as the father of a big family, with three sons: his small but well-built

Vrej, Ara the brunette, and Toros-Levon the blond. Then he foresaw his baby daughters, two gorgeous princesses, and Sara, as lovely as ever, in her role of devoted mother, pampering her daughters so proudly. Maria was a little girl looking like her mother with dark, curly hair and the most beautiful Armenian eyes. His fifth child would be a second daughter with sparking blue eyes, named after his great-grandmother, Elisabeth. 'Oh, my beautiful family!' he exclaimed aloud, overjoyed at the prospect. Then, coming back to reality, he pressed the accelerator and increased his speed, heading happily to his promising future. His chest remained swelled with happiness as his thoughts harped back to his ancestors. They would surely be proud of him. Evidently the future was bright, momentous happenstance and surprises yet to be fulfilled. He knew that it is up to the individual to grasp and cherish the moment by accepting the givens. He vowed to keep a good balance of the givens, with positive insight, with a conscious mind, and never to forget or deny his heritage and his roots!

A pauper or a prince, they all come and go, struggling for the same purpose in life: love, health beauty and freedom, enhanced through financial stability. These are pragmatic words, a concept that engulf the history and the social structure of mankind. They deem and outline the beginning and the end; they interchange and exchange, obviously they are never stamped out.

Hrant and Sara got married with the blessings and joy of their loved ones and circle of cherished friends. But one man, Christian, was close to tears, broken-hearted and regretful that he was not lucky enough to be that Swiss-Armenian prince; then Sara would have been his, but sadly it was not to be. Christian was distraught.

Sara looked like an apparition from a fairytale. Love had enlightened even more her silhouette. She looked so beautiful in her white lace and silk wedding gown. She was crowned with Edelweiss flowers, pined with fine pearls from top to toe, ready to fly, to meet her forgotten land, where women were most beautiful, passionate and dedicated; heartened and cheerful to sing and dance amidst the green meadows, proud hills, and brooks running crystal clear. She was ready, now, to jump on the fiery horse of her prince and run the chosen path forever, until the end of time.

The professor had become their guardian, likewise forever. As for the prayed-for children, surely the prince's wishes would be granted, and they, in turn, will duly arrive to grace the royal family. Patience, my Hrant, would advise our professor. Life has its own way to implement and carry out dreams. Nobody can defy nature, not even love and compassion.

Hrant my prince, let's promulgate the awesome story of love, legacy and pride, the remarkable story of two poles; overrun the history of committed and commended generations, to acquaint and unfold their bequest of hundred years, struggle of war, peace and survival, at the threshold of the twenty-first century.

Tom II

VREJ AND THE FORGOTTEN KINGDOM

Notes on sources and references:

Toros K. Topouzian, Armeniapedia

Royal Descents, Notable Kin and Printed Sources # 72 by Gary Boyd Roberts Anbytaforum: övriga ämnen: Kunglig genealogy: Diana Spencer

British Library Manuscript Collections, 96 Euston Road, London NW1 2DB

New England, Historical Genealogical Society. New England Ancestors.org

Roots Web: GEN-MEDIEVAL-L Re: DIANA

Retrieved from "http:/en.wikipedia.org/wiki/Armenia_in_India. Wikipedia is registered under the terms of GNU Free Documentation License.

Yuri Babayan

-"Sacred: books of three Faiths: Judaism, Christianity, Islam." Edited by John Reeve

-Essays by Karen Armstrong Everett Fox, FE Peters Catalogue Contribution by:

-Colin Baker Kathleen Doyle, Scot McKendrick Vrej Nersessian and Ilana Tahan

-"Marvellous to Behold Miracles in Medieval Manuscripts" by Deirdre Jackson.

-Historical Atlas of Armenia Text Garbis Armen Editing Vrej-Armen Artinian

- Claude Mutafian « Le Royaume arménien de Cilicie » The Armenian Kingdom of   Cilicia

-Amin Maalouf « Les Croisades vues par les Arabe. »

-Vahan Kurkjian. "History of Armenia, Tigran the Great" 1958.

-Richard G. Hovannisian: "Armenian Tsopk/Kharpert" "Armenian Baghesh/Bitilis" and "Taron/Mush" "Armenian Van/Vaspurakan" "The Republic of Armenia"

(4 volumes).

-Bournoutian GeorgeA (2006) A concise History of the Armenian people.

-Cambridge University Press, "Kingdom of Jerusalem."